Missing

By Andy Arnold

Acknowledgments

To my parents, Dave and Julie Arnold, for their support and for my mom helping me with proofreading and editing.

To my fellow author friend, Russ Vitrano III, for proofreading, editing my novel and providing insight.

To my Aunt Pam for also proofreading my story and providing feedback.

To Amy Kaufman for sharing her insights about having a child with Autism.

To Collin Kaufman for providing his insights about having a brother with autism.

To Chanda Telleen, for sharing insights about having a child with Downs syndrome.

To Janet Chiarito, to whom I interviewed years ago for a class project, about having a child with severe cognitive impairment.

To friends Brian Maag and Mark Janowski for consulting me on computers and technology to make my story believable. Additional thanks to Maag and Sharon Duncan for helping with formatting issues during publishing.

To my cousin Sarah Caldwell for consulting me on journalism procedures and strategies.

To John Elza for providing insights on police and FBI procedures.

To Dan Martin and Mark Beguin for consulting me about forklifts.

To Mark Beguin also for designing the cover for the book and designing my new author website.

To WriteOn Joliet group for guiding me through this process.

To professional editor Rob Bignell for his services.

To writing group head Denise Baran-Unland and her daughter, Rebekah, for their services of assisting with KDP self-publishing.

Note from Author

Hello readers. I worked for ten years in the field of special education, eight years as a teaching assistant, and two as a lead teacher. From being a one-on-one assistant for a child with severe cognitive impairment to being a resource student teacher of kids with slight learning disabilities, I have had a vast experience with the population. I have incorporated these experiences, as well as some of my own from having been a child with a slight learning disability, all into this riveting thriller of a story. One of my goals from this story is to show that while individuals with disabilities may seem very helpless and incapable of many things, they have unique abilities that would surprise many people. Also, when placed in a life and death struggle, all of us may discover abilities we never thought we had.

Section 1

Chapter 1

ndrea Meacham methodically and with focused precision chopped up the romaine lettuce as she prepared the evening meal. She was on autopilot as she juggled her numerous life responsibilities and managed her life's stressors.

She had just had an argument with her 15-year old daughter, Brittney. Fifteen-year old girls thought the whole world revolved around them! Andrea's two-year old son, Benjamin, had been cranky since he had missed his afternoon nap. He was currently occupied and being entertained by the Cartoon Network. However, at any moment she may have to run and redirect her little Energizer Bunny.

Then there was Ronald. Although he was already 18, he too may need to be redirected. He was prone to wandering or running off. Therefore, the Meachams had to have the doors locked from the inside of the house to prevent Ronald from running outside at any random time.

Andrea also fretted about her husband, who worked numerous hours, leaving much of the household duties to her. There was also her own part-time job that while providing some of her own spending money added to her stress. Her husband often did not approve of her spending or shopping habits, so she felt it was necessary to get a job of her own. Yeah, even though it was the 21st century, she felt that most of the family duties fell to her, the mom! Even though Tyler was the breadwinner, she was Suzie Homemaker. Lately, life had been frustrating since she didn't feel that she really got a break! She had her part-time job and three kids. If she wasn't making sure Ronald was getting the care he needed at school, she was feeding and tending to baby Benjamin. If she wasn't doing those things, she was attending a swim meet or other event for

Brittney. Then, of course, the household chores often fell mainly to her since Ronald and Benjamin weren't able to help. Unfortunately, Andrea also felt that many of her friends didn't want to spend much time with her this past year and a half. The reason was because of her husband's recent mistake that had brought much embarrassment to the community.

The microwave beeped signaling that the meatloaf was ready to be removed from the oven. While simultaneously setting the booster chair for Benjamin and the plates, and chopping Ronald's food, she called to Brittney, "Can I have a little help pouring drinks and rounding up Ben and Ronald!"

"I'm a step ahead of you, Mom," said a sarcastic Brittney, as she guided Ronald and Ben into the kitchen. "You don't have to use a tone with me."

"I appreciate your help. I'm just not used to having you willingly help out."

"Mom, I have a busy life too! I'm in three honors classes, band, swimming and National Honor Society. I'm not like your indentured servant!"

Andrea was about to provide a sassy comeback to put Brittney in her place but thought better of it. Why add fuel to the fire?

"Servant," chirped two-year old Benjamin.

Ronald then made his move to play with the pots and pans on the stove but Brittney strategically redirected him to the dinner table.

Just then, the horn from an approaching train blared. As if clockwork, Ronald jumped out of his seat and ran to the front door and began banging and screaming "Ahhhh, Ahhhhhhh!"

Andrea glanced at Brittney, who rolled her eyes and said, "Don't worry about it, Mom, I'll get it like I always do. Come on Ron." Brittney reluctantly but with purpose unlocked and opened the front door for her older brother.

Andrea began feeding Benjamin, as Brittney escorted Ronald out the front door. Ronald always felt that he had to watch the trains from outside. He had been fascinated by them since he was about five years old. He would rock back and forth, as the train indifferently zoomed by. It certainly did seem to have a calming influence on him.

Brittney and Ronald made their way to the end of the large backyard in this upper-middle class community. They walked around the finely landscaped bushes that lined up the back border of their yard and stood several feet away from the train tracks. The triple-track railroad ran just outside the Meacham property. The train tracks and the freight trains zooming past their backyard made for a fairly noisy night sleep and this had been one of Andrea's only issues with buying this house years earlier. However, they had gotten used to this night time noise over time.

After a few minutes of the train moving swiftly by, Andrea heard the most gut-wrenching and terrified scream she had ever heard from Brittney. Even though dramatic yelling was not uncommon for her only daughter, Andrea's gut told her that there was much more to this outburst of emotion. Something was seriously wrong.

"What's going on?" demanded Andrea as she ran out the front door and her stress level sky-rocketed. Andrea then saw Brittney lying on the ground and appeared to be groggy as if she had just woken up. "Where's Ronald?"

"Huh?" asked a confused and not very alert Brittney.

"Ronald, where is he?" shouted Andrea and her eyes darted back and forth.

As Brittney became more alert, she also became more frantic. "Oh my gosh, someone just grabbed him and ran away! They zapped me with a taser!"

Andrea then wailed uncontrollably as her worst fears about having a son like Ronald seemed to be coming true in one random moment.

* * *

"Hey, this spaghetti really hits the spot!" I exclaimed to my 27-year old daughter, Michelle.

"Well, I may not be joining Rachael Ray's staff anytime soon, but my meals are definitely a healthier alternative to Taco Bell."

My weekly "dates" with Michelle were the highlight of my existence lately. Spending time with my daughter offered an escape from my depression. Although my job occupied much of my time and kept my mind off my problems, Michelle was truly my calming influence.

"If it weren't for you, Pumpkin, I would probably make the local Taco Bell the most
profitable business around."

"Dad, I hate to tell you this, but I will be traveling to Milwaukee next week. So you
may have to find an alternate means of obtaining a healthy meal."

"Oh fine, I guess I'll have to go to the Walmart down the road from my house and buy them out of their stock of Lean Cuisine frozen dinners."

"That's *one* option."

I knew Michelle wanted to further suggest that I re-enter the dating world. However, my sweet and sensitive daughter knew that that was still a very sore subject. Since the death of my wife and 15-year old daughter, Angela, a few years ago, I was still limping through the grieving process. My job occupied my time and my relationship with Aiden and Michelle helped me get through every day. I know my surviving kids needed my support in getting over the loss of their mother and sister, but the pain was still eating me up. I did what I could for them, but how could I truly help them when I couldn't even help myself!

"You're thinking about them again, aren't you?" asked Michelle. "Dad, it's probably better to talk about it. You don't have to go through this by your..."

"I know," I exclaimed and signaled for Michelle to not say anymore. "It's just hard, because talking about it doesn't seem to help."

"Would you like some dessert?" asked Michelle sensing the futility of keeping the previous conversation on its current course.

"Nah, I'd better get going," I said. "I have a meeting early tomorrow morning."

"Ok," said a sighing Michelle. "I'll be keeping in touch with you next week. I just
worry about you."

I embraced my little girl. She had Sharon's compassion and maternal instincts. She would make a fine mother someday. Fortunately, she also inherited my drive and ambition. She was a first-year lawyer at a prestigious law firm in the city. She practiced a kind of law known as subrogation, in which lawyers help corporations recover money that they should not have had to have initially paid. That was really the best that I could understand and explain of what she did. Next week in Milwaukee, she was going to be investigating what had caused a fire at a Walmart distribution center to see if the blame could be pinned on someone else.

"Goodbye Daddy," said Michelle after I helped her place the last dirty plate in the dishwasher. "Take care of yourself and have some fun!"

"Thank you Sweetie," I said after I grabbed my coat and headed for the front door of her high-rise condo in this downtown area of this up and coming suburb.

As I drove home in my Elantra, I compartmentalized my mind and began thinking about my job. Now was not the time to reflect any more about my pain and grief. As I was lost in my thoughts about my next day's schedule, my cell phone music began playing.

"This is Graham," I said after activating the car's Bluetooth.

"Mark, this is Bingham," said my boss. "We have a kidnapping of a mentally disabled 18-year old boy."

No rest for the weary, I thought. "And the kidnapping has already crossed state lines?" I asked.

"The missing child is the son of Tyler Meacham. You are to head to the house immediately and assist the local law enforcement. If necessary, we will be deploying a C.A.R.D. team."

After being given the address of Andrea and Tyler Meacham, I again blocked out my thoughts about my personal life and focused solely on my job. I then drove to the Meacham's house with single-minded efficiency.

***

Jen Noto diligently typed away on her Mac laptop while she listened on her iPod to her favorite 80s band. She pressed forward with this task at hand since she was in no hurry to get home and risk having one of her nightmares. Her psychiatrist had her on multiple medications to control her depression. The pain she dealt with on a regular basis was something most people simply could not relate to. Many well-meaning friends had tried to tell her over the years that they understood what she was going through. That often frustrated her since they had not walked in her shoes. Having doctors always tell her that she had a chemical imbalance in her brain was also frustrating. Since this was an area of her life she simply could not control, she focused on what she did best. As she worked, the 1980s and 1990s band members from the posters perched on her wall of her apartment watched over her. At least she liked to think that people like Aerosmith and Freddy Mercury were keeping an eye and protecting her.

Starship's "We Built this City" music ringtone on her cell phone blasted without
warning and Jen noticed the I.D. of her boss, Nancy Ito.

Jen grabbed her phone, said hello and gave her boss her undivided attention, always anxious to get the jump on a big story.

"Hue, we have heard on the police scanner that there has been a major kidnapping in our town."

"Oh?" said Noto with a raised eyebrow.

"It's not just any kidnapping. The victim is an 18-year old boy with cognitive impairment. Plus, it sounds as if they have called in the FBI to assist the local police!"

"I'm all over it," said Noto. "I'm so there!"

"The boy is also the son of Tyler Meacham! Now get moving before other media
outlets get the jump on the story!"

***

As I entered the Meacham's house, I was greeted by two local police officers, Jim Anderson and Bob Ventrelli. Andrea Meacham trembled frantically, and her eyes were red from her tears. There was an elderly neighbor there caring for the toddler son so this minimized the chaos. The daughter was wide-eyed staring blankly ahead.

Ventrelli made the introductions. "This is Andrea Meacham and her daughter, Brittney. They were eating dinner with their baby brother and their older son, Ronald, who is severely disabled. When a freight train passed the house, Brittney took Ronald out to watch the train."

I nodded for this made sense. In my study of human behavior and from personal experience, kids with disabilities often had a fascination with trains.

"Someone then tased Brittney. As she turned around, she noticed that Ronald was gone. She saw the car zooming off but can't remember what the car looked like. She's just in too much shock."

"I might be able to help her," I said. "I've been trained in hypnosis techniques by the bureau and may be able to help her remember what she saw. What else do you have?"

"We've gotten a hold of Tyler Meacham, who happens to be the state treasurer. He is on his way home on an airplane right now."

"I'm aware of who Tyler Meacham is." Meacham had been involved in a scandal that involved gambling and then embezzling state funds to pay those debts over a year ago.

"We have officers interviewing extended family right now and have placed an amber alert for Ronald."

"Good. Now let me have a few minutes alone with the two Meachams to ascertain as much information as I can."

Chapter 2

Brittney shook and cried hysterically. I asked my friend and FBI colleague Ken Thompson to grab her a drink and then I sat in front of her.

"Brittney, my name is Agent Mark Graham from the FBI. I know you've been through quite a shock today. First of all, I'd like to assure you that your brother has the best team of FBI agents looking for him." She probably knew I was offering fluffed platitudes and clichés, but I did my best to put her at ease. "I'm just going to ask you a few questions. Do you feel up to that?"

She offered a weak nod.

Thompson brought her a can of Red Bull, and we got down to business. After speaking with Brittney for half an hour, I ascertained through my hypnosis technique that she had seen a person jumping out of a black SUV. This was the same person that had used the taser on Brittney and who seemingly snatched Ronald. Brittney further claimed that the person had a ski mask on and there was something else strange about this individual. However, the frustrated teenager could not remember what it was that she had thought was strange. Even though time could be of the essence, I decided not to press her on this extra detail. Hopefully it would eventually come to her. I gently patted her shoulder and thanked her for being helpful.

"If you remember anything else, please call my direct extension," I said handing her my business card.

I had quickly thumbed a text to Travis Bingham to have all police, FBI agents, and everyone else on the lookout for a suspicious looking black SUV.

When I finished speaking with Brittney, I sat down with Mrs. Meacham. I sensed that she had probably aged considerably in just a few hours. I had noticed that numerous times when I had interviewed parents of kidnapped children.

"Please find my Ronald!" blurted a frantic Mrs. Meacham. "He is so helpless and
needy! Oh my gosh, he should be taking his medication right now!"

"Everything is going to be fine," I reassured her knowing that this may be a lie. I then offered her the same words of assurance that I had for Brittney. "I'm sure you answered some of these questions already, but I am going to ask them anyway in case you remember something different this time." She did not respond so I pressed forward. After asking some of the basic questions about Ron's physical attributes and what exactly happened, I got into some of the more nitty gritty and personal questions.

"Have you noticed anyone watching this house?"

Mrs. Meacham simply shook her head.

"Any cars that repeatedly drive by? Have there been any prank calls where the caller immediately hangs up?" All of these questions pretty much yielded the same unhelpful response. I then asked what she did for a living as well as several of her relatives. She gave me some basic information which I wrote down in my notebook.

"Are there any neighbors or friends who have a grudge against you? Basically, anyone who might want to get back at you by kidnapping Ronald?"

She looked uneasy and I figured she may be thinking about the scandal involving her husband over a year ago. I certainly did not want to plant that thought in her head.

I simply said, "Mrs. Meacham, no matter how trivial or unimportant something appears, you must let me know."

"Well, even though most people like or at least tolerate Ronald, my son can be difficult. He tends to run and wander off. He will sometimes bite and scratch, especially when he's frustrated about not getting his way." She paused briefly. "He did have a paraprofessional at his school who got fired for losing his temper with Ronald. Ronald's behaviors got the best of this assistant teacher and he hit Ronald." She shuddered. "I know this young man cared for Ronald, but he had a stressful life too. When they fired him, he said he would pay my son back for ruining his life."

I inquired about the school and made a note to track down this fired assistant teacher to talk to him. "Anyone else?" I asked.

"A neighbor who lives a few blocks down the street, Mr. Peevey, also has had some issues with Ronald running into his yard and stomping through his vegetable garden. He installed a fence around his yard and said that if we did not control our child, he would have to teach him a lesson. Even though we were pissed at his comment, we shrugged it off to him being a bitter man. He was a war veteran, lived in the city for a while, and is just one of those people that trusts no one. He is also a member of the NRA. He's a jerk and a creep, but I just don't think he would kidnap anyone!"

"This is good information that I will follow up on."

"I don't want him knowing that we told on him..."

"Don't worry. I'll just tell him I'm questioning all of the neighbors and won't mention what you said. It's standard procedure anyway to canvass the area after a kidnapping."

Just then, Meacham began crying again. "I feel so helpless and I am afraid that something bad has happened to Ronald! Why is this happening?!"

Sensing I needed to put her mind at ease, I explained, "I don't think these kidnappers are violent. The good news is that they only used a non-lethal taser to temporarily incapacitate Brittney. If they were extremely dangerous, they may well have used more harmful violence to distract and get her out of the way. I am quite sure Ronald is safe."

She nodded miserably. Although my instincts did tell me that these kidnappers probably weren't violent, this was all still very disturbing. The fact that the snatch was done very methodically and quickly told me that we were probably dealing with professionals. So these people obviously meant business. Who knows what they really had in mind for this child. Tyler Meacham certainly had enemies and kidnapping one of the treasurer's children was certainly a way for them to pay him back or ransom money from him.

After we wrapped up the interview, our two tech experts, Jacob and Hamza, arrived and began planting a bug on the phone. They showed Mrs. Meacham how to activate the listening device in case the kidnappers called.

"If the kidnappers call, please keep them talking," said Agent Jacob.

Ventrelli, Anderson, Thompson, a few other agents and I got ready to begin canvassing the neighborhood to find out if anyone noticed anything.

***

Jen Noto exited her old Saturn and approached the

Meacham's house. She activated her reporter credentials and had her smartphone camera ready to take pictures of anything newsworthy. She saw the
local police cruiser parked outside the two-story Victorian house in this upper-class part of the community. The hedges and landscaping in this section of town were certainly first-rate. The people in this part of town probably paid more for landscaping than she paid a month for rent on her apartment! Jen remembered frequenting this house a year earlier when chasing for the latest lead and development on the constantly evolving Tyler Meacham scandal story.

Just then, Officers Ventrelli and Anderson walked out of the house. They were followed by a few other men wearing suits and FBI windbreakers. There was something familiar about one of the men. Oh yeah, that was Special Agent Mark Graham, the agent whose wife and younger child had been murdered. His involvement in the case complicated her getting the story! She would have to put up quite a front to get any information.

As she approached the men, Ventrelli said without even looking at her "no comment!"

When Graham saw who she was, his glare penetrated her.

"You stay away from me!" he growled. "I've got nothing to say to you!"

Noto thought of a clever comeback such as, "But you are saying something to me," then thought better of it.

"Hey guys, come on, I'm not looking for trouble."

"Of course not," Graham shot back. "You just are trouble!"

"I just want a word about what is going on!" she bellowed, not being able to think of an angle to get them to give her information.

"Here are three words," stated Graham. "Get lost forever!" With that, the men split up and began knocking on the doors of the various neighbors.

Chapter 3

Early the next morning, I headed to the bureau headquarters for the first C.A.R.D. team meeting. C.A.R.D. stood for Child Abduction Rapid Deployment. I took several deep breaths to calm myself after seeing the reporter Jen Noto. That reporter had no decency and was a sleaze. She had caused so much pain to me this past year that I could not contain my frustration from having seen her again. My rage was a boiling oven. As if I hadn't been going through enough grief the last several years! I downed another cup of coffee since I had had very little sleep the previous night. I had coordinated with my boss, Travis Bingham, to select the

C.A.R.D. team. We had scrambled through much of the night since time was of the essence. I was nominated as the team leader because of my experience and expertise in criminology. I had only caught about an hour of sleep after discussing possibilities with an FBI analyst. My anger at having seen Noto, my sleep deprivation and three cups of coffee were making me very jittery right now. After calming myself as best I could, I entered the elevator that would take me to the bureau meeting room.

Officer Ventrelli, who was heading up the police task force and acting as liaison between the local FBI and police, was present. Also present were agents Ken Thompson and Jonathon Sparks. Thompson was about my age and was a fairly thorough and professional agent. I had worked several other cases with him and trusted his instincts. I had not worked very much with Jonathon Sparks. He was nearing retirement and I had heard mixed reviews about him. Many admired him for being outspoken and willing to do what was necessary to solve a case. Some said that he was arrogant and could be very cranky to work with. About six other agents were also in attendance at this meeting. Most of us had our cups of coffee and Bingham called the meeting to order. During the meeting, I reported on my meeting the previous night with the Meachams. I cleared my throat and stated "We are dealing with the kidnapping of an 18-year old boy named Ronald Meacham. He has a disability called severe cognitive impairment." After receiving a few confused facial expressions from other agents, I clarified "He has mental retardation but that term is considered offensive and politically incorrect." Although I was a bit perturbed at the ignorance of the agents who now seemed to understand, I pressed on. "The perpetrators grabbed him from his back yard while he and his 15-year old sister were watching a train speed past their house. The kidnapper or kidnappers are very methodical and well-trained. They quickly snatched Ronald Meacham and disappeared in the car with the teenage sister only getting a brief glimpse. They tased the sister before making their getaway. I propose that he or she possibly has military or some kind of special forces training because of the stealth of the snatching. Our suspects could be people who are associated with the father, Tyler Meacham. He certainly has plenty of enemies. Using state funds to pay off gambling debts certainly has people at the capitol ticked off. Then there is the mob boss, Louie Connelli. Meacham never paid off all of his gambling debts to him. Connelli certainly has the means of having police or military personnel on his payroll. I believe he may be our prime suspect.”

“However, there are also seemingly other people that are angry with the son, Ronald Meacham,” interjected Ventrelli. “A paraprofessional at the school where the son attended hit the kid and then threatened him. We will be talking to the school where the punk assistant attended and getting his information very soon. Then there is also the neighbor, Mr. Peevey, who made threatening comments to the kid. We tried questioning him last night, but he did not answer his door. Mr. Jake Peevey was in the special forces division in Afghanistan. He was given a dishonorable discharge because of having a psychological breakdown. He returned home and inherited a vast amount of wealth from his parents. Some people from town thought that he may have killed them in order to inherit their money. He is mentally unbalanced, so I would not put anything past him. In many ways, he does fit the profile of our kidnapper. He may have even killed the boy for stomping through his garden, and stashed his body somewhere.” Everyone gasped. “Unfortunately, without a warrant, we could not force our way into his house. We are currently working on getting a warrant.”

“Indeed,” said Mr. Bingham. “We will immediately check our Violent Criminal Apprehension Program (VICAP) and other databases for anyone else with a military or special forces training with a criminal background in the area. I want Graham to accompany you, Officer Ventrelli, as you question the former school employee and the neighbor.” Bingham then went onto designate the other interviewing assignments to the other members of the team and then called for a debriefing meeting at 1 p.m.

As Ventrelli and I entered the elevator, Jonathon Sparks followed us into the elevator. Sparks said to Ken Thompson, "Too bad Bingham is only sending you to interview Tyler Meacham. We should have a whole team of agents prying through his financial records and emails. Bingham is too much of a politician. He's been eying political office for a long time."

Not wanting to get into a debate about my boss' intentions with this man, I turned the conversation into a philosophical one. "What a shame that someone would kidnap a kid like Ronald who is so needy. I have no patience or tolerance for anyone who preys upon the weak. I'd like to beat the crap out of whoever did this!"

Ventrelli and Sparks both nodded their heads.

"People are evil today," said Ventrelli. "I've seen too much of the dark side of life in my 20 years on the force."

We then exited the elevator and Ventrelli and I headed toward Brooks Valley High School.

***

Ventrelli and I entered Ronald's school and got the name of the paraprofessional who had hit and then further threatened Ronald. We interviewed the principal, Ronald's teacher, and several members of the staff who had daily contact with Ronald. Ronald's classroom was called the multi-needs room and serviced students who had extreme needs. Most of the students were in wheel-chairs. One of the students was being fed by a feeding tube. Some of the students were in devices that I think were called standers. I guess it helped stretch them out and use muscles that they wouldn't normally use. I certainly didn't have time or need to inquire about all of the methods they used for these students, so I stayed focused on the task at hand. In another situation, I would have been fascinated to learn about the techniques used to assist people of this population. In fact, in high school I had considered going into the field of special education until I had chosen law enforcement. I made my rounds, and Ventrelli and I interviewed all of the staff in the room. None of the staff had seen anything unusual or seemed to have any motive for hurting Ronald. They all agreed that he was a challenging student but overall was very lovable. The other paraprofessionals in Ronald's class seemed like caring and compassionate women. One lady said, "Oh, he was so lovable. He loved to playfully shoot people in the hallways and had this adorable smile. I think he knew more than he let on."

"What did you think of his one-one-one aide, Joe Hammonds?" I asked.

"He overall was a nice guy. However, there was just something a little off about him. He gave me the creeps at times."

Officer Ventrelli and I left the school and tracked down Joe Hammonds and found that he was working at the local supermarket. Fred, the store manager, called the stocky young man into the office.

"Please take a seat," Fred said.

"Yes, sir," said Joe Hammonds eying Ventrelli and me with suspicion. "What can I do for you gentleman?"

"Hello, I am Special Agent Mark Graham with the FBI."

Hammond's face paled slightly. This was definitely a normal reaction when someone learned they were being interviewed by the FBI.

"And I'm Detective Ventrelli from the Brooks Valley Police Department. We just have a few questions to ask you."

"Questions for me? Ok! What do you want to know?"

With a masters in criminal psychology and extensive training and experience in reading people, my gut was telling me that this guy was innocent. However, I'd been fooled before. Sometimes the best criminals could mask their emotions and even fool a lie detector test.

"Does the name Ronald Meacham mean anything to you?" Ventrelli asked.

Hammond's face went from concerned to fairly angry. "Yeah, that retard got me fired from my job and ruined my life!"

"Watch your mouth, Hammond!" said the store manager. "We don't tolerate disrespecting groups of people with talking that way. That violates company police and our ethics code!"

"My apology sir," said Hammond.

"Tell us about what happened at the school that caused him to ruin your life," I said.

"Why do you want to know?" said Hammond. "This is just plain weird!"

"Let us ask the questions. I'll ask again. What happened at the school that caused him to ruin your life?"

"I was good to that kid. I was his one-one-one teacher aide and I helped him get through each day. I helped change his diaper, cut up his food at lunch, helped him with putting his coat on and tutoring him. Heck, I even came up with the behavior plan of having him use the vacuum cleaner after completing each task!"

"The vacuum cleaner?" I queried and then worried that I might have been encouraging him to get off topic.

"Yeah, Ronald was always happiest with a vacuum cleaner in his hands. He could go all day with vacuuming if you let him. So, it was my idea to use the vacuuming as a reward."

"Hey, this kid should come and clean my house!" mused the store manager,
probably to ease the tension of the moment.

"Ok, but back to how he ruined your life," stated Ventrelli.

"Yeah, so I was good to him, but man, he was a freakin handful! He hit me, spit on me, and even bit me a couple of times. One day, I just snapped. I had had a rough evening here at the store and Ronald was pushing my every button at school. He's smarter than people give him credit for. He had just thrown a cup of juice on me, and I slapped him. I was fired on the spot! In fact, I was arrested

24

for hitting a kid with special needs. I already spent a night in jail! Man, I was studying to be a special education teacher. After my university found out about what I had done, I was advised to not continue the program."

"Where were you last night at 6 p.m.?" I asked.

Again looking confused, Hammonds replied, "I was at my apartment playing video games. Why are you asking me these questions? What the heck! Should I be calling a lawyer?"

"You can do that," said Ventrelli. "But that will just make you look guilty."

"Guilty of what?" stammered Hammonds. "What's going on?"

"Just answer our questions!" said Ventrelli raising his voice.

Even the store manager now seemed to be feeling a bit uncomfortable. I guess it was my time to play "the good cop," so to speak. "We are not accusing you of anything. We just need information, so please answer our questions. We just need information. Do you have an alibi for last night?"

"Wait, I thought you said I was not being accused of anything!"

"Just answer the question," I advised using a soothing but firm tone.

"Ah, no, my roommate was out of town and my girlfriend was at work."

"So no one can corroborate your story," I stated.

"I suppose not. Please man, tell me what this is all about. My life really has been ruined by what Ronald did, and having you guys questioning me about it here at the store only adds to my stress and anxiety. I already spent a night in jail for hitting him!

I've been clean since. Heck, other than that incident, I've had a clean record! Please, I can't go back to jail!"

Hammonds then looked like he might begin to cry. I really did not have much sympathy for this guy who had struck a kid with severe cognitive impairment. Still, it seemed like he was probably an overall good guy that had made one very bad decision under stress. There was a part of me that wanted to use my power to continue to make him sweat and keep him unbalanced. However, I figured that was unethical at this point. Full disclosure was in order.

"Ronald Meacham was kidnapped last night," I explained.

Hammonds' eyes widened and he looked like he was on the verge of a complete panic attack.

"Relax," Ventrelli added. "Although you are not a suspect yet, you are a person of interest since you do have a motive for hurting Ronald and your former principal did hear you threaten Meacham."

"Man, I made one bad mistake. I would never do something to really hurt him."

"So you say," said Ventrelli. "I have never met a guilty person who admitted to committing a crime."

"I think I should get a lawyer!" stammered Hammonds.

"There is no need for that at this time," I said. "We have asked you everything we needed. You are not the main suspect but a person of interest. Just don't think about leaving town."

***

Jen Noto sat across from Suzie Ito to discuss the blockbuster kidnapping story and how to get a jump on the other media outlets.

"I'm at my wit's end!" blurted a frustrated Jen Noto. "The man hates me, and I probably could not pay him a million dollars to let me tag along. If he catches me following him, he'll probably find some excuse to have me locked up in a federal prison."

"Well, you did breach numerous journalism ethics when pursuing his murdered family story," Ito reasoned. "You can't say you really blame the man."

Jen's eyes widened in response to Ito's being concerned about ethics. "I don't blame him. In fact, if the situation was reversed, I would hate me too."

"However," said Ito pressing forward, "we still need to get an inside scoop and you are the best journalist for the job. This is a challenge, but you have to figure out some way to get Graham to trust you."

"So I guess I have to feign remorse and get him to buy it?" suggested Noto.

"Yes, do whatever it takes, but think of something quickly," stated Ito.

Noto then left the office with numerous thoughts firing all over her head. How could she get Graham to buy her remorse? Huh, maybe this was why she was so depressed all the time. Perhaps it was not simply a chemical imbalance in her brain. Maybe she hated herself for always doing whatever it took to get a story. How badly did she really want this story? Ok, focus Noto. Do what you have to do!

Just then her smartphone rang as she exited the news building and headed toward the parking lot. It was her mom! Feeling a mixture of frustration but also concern, she answered the phone. "Hi Mom! What's up?"

"Hey, it's good to hear your voice. Especially since you never call and rarely answer your phone!"

Jen inhaled for this was an argument she usually had with her mom. She took another breath hoping this would calm her nerves and give her the necessary patience. "Mom, I am very busy with my job! I want to be able to talk and see you more, but my career takes up most of my time."

"Your job is more important than your family?"

"That's not fair!"

"Like it's fair that you never visit?"

Jen bit her tongue hard to resist a scream. Although empathy often did not come easy for Jen, she knew that laying blame was one of her mom's symptoms. "Mom, this Saturday I will try to visit you. I may have to cancel, but I will do my best."

"Thank you Hon! By the way, are there any men in your life?"

No Mom. I am married to my work. "Bye Mom. I love you and will talk to you Saturday."

Jen quickly clicked off before getting trapped in another one of her mom's emotional traps. Her mom did know how to push her buttons. Jen had battled self- esteem issues since high school. Although she was a cute girl and had been a cheer leader, she had not had much luck with guys. Guys were drawn to her, but she was so controlling and had to have everything her way all the time. Maybe that was the result of dealing with an alcoholic mother. She snapped herself out of her thoughts. For now, she had to decide how to get Mark Graham to trust her and allow her access to the case.

Chapter 4

Agent Ken Thompson entered the Pennsylvania capitol, flashed his credentials a few times and finally entered the office of Tyler Meacham. Meacham was typing away at his computer.

"May I have a word with you Mr. Meacham?" Thompson asked as he entered the office.

"Well, it will have to be quick," said Meacham. "I have a meeting in about five minutes."

"You are aware of your son being kidnapped?" asked Thompson.

"Yes, and I am quite upset about it! That's why I'm wondering why you are here and not out looking for him!"

"Hey, we need to interview all members of the immediate family. Most kidnappings occur by family members."

"So you think I kidnapped my son?"

"Right now, I – we –have not ruled anything out. We are looking at all angles and
letting the facts dictate our next moves."

"So what do you want to ask?" asked Meacham.

"I'd really like to see your financial records to ascertain about your many enemies."

"I'd really not like to revisit that area of my life," said Meacham.

"Even if doing so might help us find your son? I find it a little strange that you're still working even though your son was kidnapped last night."

Looking like he was about to cry, Meacham said, "Hey, after what I did, I don't have much leeway in getting time off, even for a family crisis. I feel horrible about what I did and even worse about my boy being kidnapped. Do you think Connelli could be behind this?"

"Again, that's what we'd like to find out. You haven't paid all of your debts to him,
have you?"

"Not yet. Please, here are my records. I've got to go. Do what you need to do!"

***

M s. Smith glanced over her autism classroom silently observing everything going on. Each of her students were engaged in his or her work centers awaiting the command to "check schedule." She felt truly lucky and blessed to teach in this prestigious autism program in a small town in eastern Maine. This up-and-coming suburb had numerous Victorian style homes, a high school that the town rallied behind and several mom-and-pop shops. The school itself was a state-of-the art facility that accommodated all students' needs. They had a first-rate computer lab, numerous lap-tops and iPads in every classroom and even a laundry room and kitchen for the students with special needs to utilize. Birches Elementary School was named after a poem written by the famous poet, Robert Frost. The name was appropriate because of the many trees and forests in the area around the town. The only location issue with this school was the forest directly next to it. Her biggest fear was that one of her students might decide to play hide and seek amongst the trees.

She glanced across the classroom and spotted the computer work station, which did not have a supervising paraprofessional.

"No YouTube, Adam!" she stated calmly but firmly.

30

Young blond-headed Adam Aaron shot her daggers. Fortunately he chose to follow her directive without further defiance. That was a relief since Adam was prone to meltdowns or temper tantrums. Although his autism severely affected his ability to learn and function like most people, in many ways he was very smart. In fact, his intelligence truly sparkled when he was in front of a computer. He could access any website, delete or move any file, or hack into any program. When he printed and sent random Internet material to the district office, that was one thing. However, downloading inappropriate websites and hacking into the district's classified files posed a larger problem. Even though his hacking and other computer exploits were usually not done with malicious intent, they still messed up the computers and created problems. He had all these natural abilities on computers without the basic intelligence to harness and control those abilities.

The topper to this issue occurred when the technician for the district visited Ms. Smith's classroom and installed an Internet block on the computer. The technician had said "There, if that kid gets passed this block, I will hire him to work on my staff!" Sure enough, Adam had broken through the block within minutes.

Now it was simply a matter of watching Adam like a hawk whenever he was on a computer. In fact, Ms. Smith had had the creative challenge of devising a Boardmaker picture directing Adam to not hack into computers. This software, which was a program for making picture cards, was ideal for autism students. Children with autism are very visual so picture cards that tell them to have "quiet mouth," "quiet hands," and "no hitting" were often far more effective than simply saying these things. Ms. Smith had debated about how to find a picture on Boardmaker that would be good for saying "No hacking!" She ended up just placing a picture of a computer and having the text say "Only play games and work on computer." Adam's computer genius skills were amazing, since academically he was really only on the level of a preschooler. His social skills also were very below average. Computers truly unlocked his potential.

At the end of the current center, Ms. Smith announced, "Green work is all done, it is time to check schedule."

The students went through the process of checking their schedules. The numerous paraprofessionals or teaching assistants stood back without directing the students. Ms. Smith had trained her assistants to not prompt or give directions to the students unless they absolutely had to guide them. The philosophy was to teach the students to be as independent as possible.

The students then lined up for their daily walk. The class exited the classroom and walked along the newly tiled and exquisitely designed hallways of this state-of-the-art school building. They passed the glass-walled library that was currently full of mainly studious and eager-to-learn fifth graders. These students were either researching on the computer, working on school work, or silently reading or checking out books. In the corner, a librarian read to a group of kindergartners.

Ms. Smith led her class out the front door of the building and onto a sidewalk leading away from the neighboring forest. The birds were chirping, and the breeze cascaded off their faces on this beautiful September day.

As the children and adults briskly walked along, everything was going smoothly. Suddenly a small explosion erupted, and complete chaos ensued. The children all scattered, and Ms. Smith screamed "Guys, grab your students!" One of the students ran in front of a moving car and two of the paraprofessionals leapt into the road and pulled young Larry out of harm's way. Ms. Smith assisted another paraprofessional in convincing her child to come out from inside a bush. After redirecting the students to the sidewalk and calming them down amidst the chaos several minutes later, Mrs. Penny began yelling from the forest, "I can't find Adam! Help, help, Adam is gone!" Ms. Smith felt as if her heart skipped ten beats at that moment!

The kidnapper ran stealthily through the woods with Adam tucked under her arm. That could not have gone smoother! The class had taken its daily walk right on schedule. After throwing the flash grenade, Adam had darted for the woods as predicted. She and her boss had observed that behavior from Adam. Fortunately Adam's paraprofessional had assisted in rescuing the boy who ran in front of the car. If that boy had been killed, that would have been unfortunate collateral damage. The kidnapper would not have lost any sleep over that but she had the sense that her boss would have been in a major funk over such an occurrence. She would have had no problem with harming or even killing the teenage girl, Brittney, before the last kidnapping. However, her boss had been very clear about only tasing the younger sister. He was such a softy! However, he was her employer, so he called the shots, for now. In due time, she would assert her authority and probably eliminate him along with everyone else. For now, though, acting as a subordinate served her purpose to give the boss the illusion of being in control. Adam was now asleep from the drug she had inserted from the syringe into his bloodstream. The woman then handed the boy to the two men in the vehicle, and they swiftly vacated the premises.

Chapter 5

Officer Ventrelli and I knocked harshly on the door of Mr. Jake Peevey's one-story house after receiving the warrant from the Brooks Valley judge. We may need to force our way into his house

if he did not answer again. While most of the other houses on the block had multiple stories, Peevey spent his money on his yard. The overgrown shrubbery and pine trees blocking the view of the house from the road clearly gave the impression that this man did not want to be disturbed.

"What do you want?" bellowed the man from behind the peep hole. My hunch about him was apparently correct.

"Mr. Peevey, this is Officer Ventrelli from the Brooks Valley Police Department."

"And I am Agent Mark Graham from the FBI."

Ventrelli and I showed our badges and I was sure that would intimidate the man into a better attitude. It worked with most people.

"We just want to ask you a few questions. May we come in?" I asked.

"Quit waving your fascist badges at me. I haven't done anything!"

"We didn't say that you did," I continued. "We just need to ask you a few questions."

I considered explaining about the kidnapping, but I just couldn't resist making this guy sweat a little.

"Unless you guys have a warrant, I want you off my property!" I heard a click on the other end. "I am an excellent shot and have no problem putting a round in your head. This is my property, and I want you off of it!"

Ventrelli and I both stepped away from the door and drew our own weapons. I'd been in life and death situations before, but this situation was unexpected. So I took a deep breath and spoke professionally.

"Calm down Mr. Peevey. There has been a kidnapping of a child in your neighborhood. We're talking to all of the neighbors. Plus, think about it! If you shoot at us, you'll be locked in a federal prison for shooting an FBI agent. Believe me, you'll get no preferential treatment for shooting a fed! Trust me, a federal prison is worse than the military stockade you already spent time in."

Peevey grunted uneasily.

"Plus," added Bob Ventrelli, "you'll be a cop killer. They won't take too kindly to holding my killer while you are temporarily locked up here in Brooks Valley. The cops will rough you up until you are taken into federal custody. Oh and by the way, the other prisoners will see you as a suspect for the kidnapping that has occurred in our town. Hmmm. Perpetrators of crimes against children often get the worst treatment in jails and prisons."

Peevey seemed to have cooler thoughts prevail as he holstered his weapon, threw open the door and acquiesced. "Ah, come on in and don't brush up against my walls. I just repainted them a week ago," said this 42-year old war veteran.

I was relieved not to have to show Peevey our warrant. Andrea Meacham had seemed scared of him and I didn't want to bring her any other unnecessary trouble. After having Peevey hand over his sidearm, we followed him into his kitchen. I contemplated doing a body search which would have been my right since he had pulled his weapon on us, but I figured we had talked enough sense into him so that he would not do anything stupid. Plus, I wanted him to calm down so he would give us whatever information he might have.

After explaining about the kidnapping, we asked Peevey if he knew Ronald Meacham.

"Yeah, I know him. He's like a mindless animal that wonders into my yard and
picks leaves off my bushes and trees."

"Watch it Peevey! He does have a disability and is a human being after all!" Ventrelli firmly stated.

"Oh, get over it. You are just like the boy's parents and everyone else in society always making excuses. That boy just needs a little old fashioned discipline!"

"Is it possible you provided that discipline by snatching him from his family?" I
asked.

"I haven't kidnapped anyone!" sneered Peevey. "Why would anyone want that kid? It seems all he does is eat, sleep and poop!"

"Where were you two nights ago at 9 p.m. when we canvassed the neighborhood and knocked on your door?" asked Ventrelli.

"Not that it's any of your business, but I was asleep. I go to sleep at 8 p.m. and wear ear plugs so as to not be bothered by the sounds of the darn teenage kids that play music late at night."

"Do you mind if we take a look around?" I asked him again hoping we wouldn't have to produce our warrant.

"Yeah, I mind, but go ahead. I've got nothing to hide!"

After a thorough search where we did not find Ronald, we gave him a business card and asked him to contact both of us if he saw the boy. However, I did not feel we could count on this character. As we exited his yard, I kicked over a bunch of his flowers in his tulip garden. I simply could not resist!

Just then, my phone buzzed that a text message was coming through. I looked and it was from Bingham. Autistic boy from school in Maine kidnapped while in school. Possible connection. Report for immediate C.A.R.D. meeting.

***

My head was ready to explode! Bingham had just announced that a young boy with autism had been kidnapped in Maine. Local law enforcement in the small town of Mapleville, Maine, were coordinating with the local FBI office to resolve that kidnapping because of the possible connection. I was going to be deployed to Maine the next day to investigate. Two kidnappings in a matter of days involving two kids with severe special needs! This was suddenly one of the strangest cases I had ever worked. I was going to have to visit the school where this Adam Aaron attended and interview every staff member and even perhaps several of the students. I was also going to have to retrace and analyze the ingress and egress of the kidnapper.

"Graham, may we talk just for a second?" a female voice that I despised said, rudely awakening me from my disturbed thoughts, as I exited the headquarters building and walked through the parking lot.

I turned my head and then began quickly walking toward my car to elude Ms. Jen Noto from the Brooks Valley Gazette. As if I wasn't upset enough at the moment, seeing this woman who had hurt me quite badly while pursuing the story on my murdered family increased my stress level exponentially. I bolted past her without a word.

"Graham, I know what you think of me, and I totally don't blame you. I admit, I was completely wrong with pretending I was a former friend of your wife just to gain access to her personal belongings. I would do anything to take back what I did! But all I can do is sincerely apologize. However, we might be able to help each other out."

I turned toward her after I unlocked my car and felt my anger reaching its absolute boiling point. "How can you possibly help me?" I asked through clenched teeth as I grabbed her forearm.

"Hey, let go! You are hurting me!"

I let go. Someone like this opportunist could use me grabbing her to her advantage. I would not put it past her to have someone recording that and then using it to blackmail me into helping her. She would demand me giving her information or she would go to the cops or the media.

She actually surprised me by what she said next. "I actually kind of deserved that," she said while rubbing her forearm. "I probably deserve a lot more for the journalistic low I hit when I wrote your wife's diary entries in the paper and suggested she might have been having an affair."

"I don't believe for a second that you are really sincere," I said.
"You are an excellent actress and master manipulator. You will do anything for a story!"

"You are basically right," said Noto. "I will do almost anything for a story.
However, I think maybe we can help each other out."

"Yeah right! How can you help me out?"

"Well, you know I am great at getting information out of people," said Noto. "Also, I hear things. If you and I work together, we may be able to find both of these kidnapped kids."

"How did you know there were two kids?"

"I told you. I hear things."

I stared at her in a way that practically threatened her to give more information.

"Well, I actually made an educated guess. When I saw several agents breaking for this meeting and with the look on your face, I used inductive reasoning to guess that there had been another kidnapping. Thank you for confirming my beliefs."

She actually said it without much cockiness. Still, she was slick!

"It's not unusual for a journalist and FBI agent to work together. I'll use my investigative journalist skills, and you use your skills. I'll get the story, and you will get the kids. We both win."

"Not a chance! There is no way I am trusting you after humiliating the memory of my wife! Get out of here or I'll make your life miserable!"

***

Adam Aaron squirmed, as he was in that stage between a sound sleep and being awake. Something was indeed off with the world. He moaned and squirmed in his sleep and finally woke up. He farted, as he noticed he was in a strange bed and different room. The anxiety he felt was unlike anything he had ever experienced. All of a sudden, he felt extreme calm shoot through him. He often felt this peace a few minutes after he took the pill his mom always gave him with his breakfast. Despite his calm sensation, he knew everything was way off! His eyes darted around the room, as he took everything in.

Just then the door knob began to turn. Adam's brain told him that he wanted to throw something or kick and scream, but he just felt too calm. The door opened, and a tall man with blond hair and glasses entered carrying a breakfast tray toward the bed.

"Good morning Adam," the man said in a very kind and compassionate tone. He set up a TV tray. "I made you your favorite breakfast bud." It was scrambled eggs with melted cheese glazed over it and bacon on the side.

As Adam sat up and began eating, the man continued talking. The man told Adam what his name was and said, "I am going to be taking care of you for now on. I am going to be like a dad in the mornings and nights. I will be your school teacher during the day."

He then pulled out a square board with small square pictures on it. It was just like those pictures they used at his school.

Pointing to each picture, the man said, "First you may eat breakfast, then brush your teeth, then you may play on my computer." Adam felt a rush of further happiness knowing that he would be able to play on the computer. "Then it will be time for you to go to your new school."

"Momma, Andrew?" asked Adam expectantly.

The man seemed a bit sad but then continued "Not for a while. You have a new home for a while."

"No new home. Want Mom and Dad, want Mom and Dad. Want Andrew," stammered Adam.

"In a few days, bud. Listen to this story." The man began reading a story to Adam. "I have a new home and new school. My new teacher and other people will be taking care of me now. I must follow their rules, and I will have fun. I will have two new friends staying with me at this school. My new school will be different, but this is okay. My new school and home are fun!"

Chapter 6

On my plane ride to Maine, I had a lot on my mind.

Besides the case, my discussion with Noto made my mind go back to thoughts that I had tried to forget. I had been super pissed when Noto had gone through my wife's diary and suggested that she had been having an affair. There was no way Sharon would have cheated on me. Our life together was as storybook of a relationship as you can get. I had been a star athlete in high school so everyone had always thought that I would date only the cool girls. I had chosen Sharon Caldwell, who was considered a misfit by much of the student body. I had approached her as she sat alone in the cafeteria. Initially, she had not shown much interest. She probably figured I was playing some sort of joke by talking to her. After I had broken down her walls, our romance and relationship soared.

So anyway, Noto had read and written a passage in the diary that had implied that she was having an affair and that perhaps her lover was trying to keep the relationship silent. As much as I did not believe Noto's accusations, that part of her diary had indeed intrigued me if not concerned me. Perhaps that was why I was doubly angry about Noto publicly exposing it. It had read, "*I have to meet my neediest patient, Armon Luck, away from the office. I am deeply concerned since this is against protocol and highly irregular.*" Another passage had read "*Armon Luck is bringing out emotions in me I never thought I had. I feel the need and obligation to meet him.*" Sharon had been extremely dedicated to her job as a psychiatrist. She had bent over backwards for all of her patients, so I'm sure this was legit. However, there was something strange about this Armon Luck bringing out "emotions in me I never thought I had." At least she hadn't said she had feelings for him, but what did she mean by what she had said? Why was she meeting with him outside her office? The police and FBI, not including me, had interrogated Armon Luck, but the man was very sick and in the psychiatric hospital. Supposedly, he had been in his room, according to nurses, while my wife and daughter were being murdered. I finished drinking my soda just as the plane began its descent to land.

As I exited the airplane in Augusta, Maine, I was promptly greeted by an officer named Carl Soldano. Officer Soldano was less than friendly with me, but I didn't care. This case was heating up, and I did not have much time for pleasantries. Now that there were two kids with special needs missing, the urgency had sky-rocketed. I definitely needed to interview mob boss Louie Connelli, who had reason to be ticked off with Tyler Meacham. What connection he might have with Adam Aaron and his family, I did not know. After I was done with officer Soldano interviewing Connelli, I would be analyzing the scene of the kidnapping at Birches Elementary School. Then I would be meeting with Adam Aaron's parents with the lead detective in that town.

"This ain't good," said Soldano. "You really don't know what tree you're barking up against by interviewing Connelli."

"Hey, when I became an FBI agent, I knew what I was getting into. I didn't take
the job to make friends."

"Yeah, but I've been covering the Connelli family for a while. He knows his limits in our city. We have had a hard time pinning any real crimes on him, but he does make people disappear."

"That's why I have to question him," I said irritably. "He may be holding two very needy children against their will."

"I don't think he would go after any children. He has four kids himself and seems to have principles. Well, I just know he doesn't like the FBI and people he doesn't know questioning him. You come around accusing him of kidnapping children, he won't be happy."

"Right now, I'm not happy either. Two children are missing and I cannot stand it when people mess with kids!"

"All right man, I'm just trying to warn you."

At about 2 p.m., we pulled into a huge health club. Soldano showed me his iPad that contained Connelli's itinerary.

"This is about the time that Connelli gets done with his workout. He's gonna be pissed."

This state of the art facility had numerous free weights and universal gym machines. The place was fairly busy for a week-day afternoon. That's life in the big city.

Connelli sweated profusely as he peddled rapidly on a stationary bike while listening to his iPod.

"Connelli, I have an FBI agent who needs to talk to you," said Soldano. Just as I approached him with my credentials ready, two muscular Italian men emerged from nowhere and dressed in sweat outfits.

"Whoa, the boss has a tight schedule Officer Soldano. Plus, he hasn't done anything," the bigger of the two men said.

"Chill out Vito," said Soldano. "This is a federal agent and my hands are tied. He just has a few questions."

"What the hell does the FBI want with me?" growled Connelli. "I haven't done anything. I am a prominent businessman and you two are embarrassing me."

"We're not embarrassing you!" I said angrily. "You're embarrassing yourself! I just have routine questions and you and your two little friends are jumping to conclusions. Only people who have something to hide become so defensive."

The man named Vito got in my face and asked Connelli if he should teach me a lesson.

"Seriously Bobby Vito," said Soldano. "You really want to ignite a war with the feds?"

Maybe Soldano was not so bad after all.

"All right Lezza and Vito, back down," said Connelli. "I'll talk to these two gentlemen."

Connelli helped himself off the bike and began wiping off with the white towel as the five of us walked over to one of the tables at the end of the facility.

I began. "So, I know you have had a past history with Tyler Meacham. Does that name ring a bell?"

"Why should it?"

"Several thousand in gambling debt that he owes you?"

"Ah, I remember that creep! He is a deadbeat that owes me money."

"Yet you didn't have him whacked. That was mighty generous of you."

"Who says I have hurt anyone? In this country, I am innocent until proven guilty. Plus, the man has kids. I have a special place for kids. I would not hurt someone with kids."

This creep was choosing his words very carefully so as to not say anything incriminating. He definitely knew his rights. "Were you aware that his 18-year old son with special needs went missing a few days ago?" I asked.

"Oh yeah, I did read about that. Hah, and you think I kidnapped the boy?"

"Well, you certainly have the motive, and the means."

Connelli looked angry again. "Like I said, I have compassion for kids. Though I don't like everybody, I would never hurt someone who has kids and especially kidnap a kid. I've got principles."

"Do you have an alibi for last Thursday evening when he was kidnapped?" I asked. "Last Thursday, oh yeah, I was at the theater with my wife."

"Do you have your ticket stub?"

"It's back at my office at the restaurant."

"I'm going to need to see it and get the name of at least two people who can verify that you were there."

"This is really messing up my schedule. I have a meeting with three other business owners at 3."

44

"Well, you'd better let them know that you might be late," I said.

"Do you know who you are dealing with?" he said while standing.

"Right now, I don't care if you are the Pope! Another child has been kidnapped and since you're on the list of possible enemies of one of the fathers, I need your cooperation."

While he looked ready to fight and his two henchmen inched closer, he then calmed down again. Several people in the facility began paying attention to this encounter. Connelli seemed self-conscious about people staring at him. I guess the businessman in him took control and he did not want the negative publicity of him fighting in public with an FBI agent.

"All right man. You are just doing your job. Let me shower and make some calls. Then you can follow me to my restaurant, and I'll get you what you need."

***

After Louie Connelli's last meeting for the day, he summoned Bobby Vito and Benny Lezza into his office.

"I figured you'd want to talk to us," said Vito.

"Yeah, what makes you say that?" asked Connelli.

"Hey, I know you don't like surprises and accusations from unexpected visitors, like that FBI agent today."

Connelli nodded. "You know me too well."

"Hey, I've got your back, man."

"Yeah, have you found out everything you can about this Mark Graham?"

"Yes, we don't know where he lives yet but we know where he works."

"Very good. I think you know what your next assignment is then."

"I do," said Vito.

"But boss," stammered a trembling Benny Lezza. "The man is a fed. Are you sure you want to mess with him?"

Connelli then gave a stare to Lezza that would have made even the most thick skinned and brave men tremble.

"If it weren't for my sister loving you so much, you'd be off my payroll so quick man. Now don't ask anymore stupid questions. I don't always make an honest buck and I do have some negotiation tactics that have questionable legality. Yes, and I have been able to make people disappear from time to time. However, I do have principles. When someone accuses me of something so heinous as kidnapping, I take offense. So, this guy needs to learn a lesson. There will be no proof that will lead him back to me. Don't kill him, just rough him up severely."

"Consider it done," said a determined Vito.

***

Officer Carl Soldano and I drove into the fairly affluent Mapleville community. We visited Birches Elementary School and analyzed the crime scene. I interviewed Ms. Smith and her aides who had all reported a mysterious bang and noticed a flash. There was a large forest next to the school and a gravel path where we determined that the kidnapper allegedly entered onto the school grounds. There was a road on the other end of the forest where the kidnapper probably had a getaway vehicle. There were more than likely more than one kidnapper. I'm figuring that one person made the snatch while someone or several people drove the getaway vehicle. The footprints on the soil were obviously now gone since the kidnapping, but fortunately the local forensics team had taken pictures of the footsteps the kidnapper had used to enter and exit the scene. What struck me was that the kidnappers obviously knew exactly when the class was going to be taking its daily walk. How could they have known this? It was kind of like with Ronald Meacham; the kidnappers seemingly knew when he'd be going outside to watch the train. After numerous interviews with staff and administrators, no-one had seen anyone or noticed anything unusual prior to the kidnapping. There was apparently no-one seen watching the school. So how did they get the class schedule? One idea was that someone inside the school had helped the kidnappers, but that seemed unlikely. What also concerned me was that apparently a flash grenade had been used this time. After Ronald's kidnapping, I had considered that the kidnappers had military training. Now that seemed even more likely. What also was noteworthy was that these people were apparently very well-financed.

After visiting the school, we drove to a beautiful, two-story blue house, that belonged to the Aarons. Several cars were present as there were apparently several family and friends supporting this family. As we entered the house, we were first greeted by a man in his early forties and wearing a business suit. He introduced himself as Ben Aaron. We then met Alice Aaron, a petite woman with blonde hair, glasses and jeans. Her eyes were red; I was sure she had been crying constantly.

"Please come in gentleman," said Alice Aaron. "Can I get you anything? Coffee, tea?"

"We're good ma'am," I said. "We'll get right to business so we can bring your boy back."

The woman grimaced and looked as if she might begin crying again. "Please do! I miss him so much and feel so helpless."

"Don't you worry, ma'am. I just want to inform you that you have the top team of FBI agents looking for Adam. We will not rest until we find him!" I knew not to promise that we'd bring him back. However, I had to assure this frantic woman that we would do everything humanly possible to return her child.

Just then an elderly couple walked in.

"These are my parents. They're helping out with our other child, Andrew. I'm just having a hard time being the mom I need for my other son since I'm so worried about Adam!"

The grandparents introduced themselves and then went back to fixing dinner.

I started with the basic questions such as if they had seen anyone driving past the house over and over, anyone watching the house, or anything suspicious. Neither of the Aarons had noticed anything. As with Ronald Meacham, there had been absolutely no ransom demands as of yet. Therefore, my hunch was telling me that this was not about money. This perpetrator, if it was indeed the same kidnapper for both boys, apparently had some personal connection to kids with special needs. Also, this child apparently had no enemies. Aside from a few behaviors typical of children with autism, he was apparently well-liked by his peers and neighbors. Alice Aaron showed us a picture of him in his baseball uniform for his Special Olympics team. She showed us other pictures of the boy with his twin brother, Andrew. One of them showed Adam kissing his twin when the two children were younger.

"I can tell the brothers are identical. May I please meet Andrew?"

"Sure," said Ben Aaron. "Andrew, someone would like to meet you."

The ten-year old boy walked in very somberly. He resembled his brother by having wavy, blond hair and seemed like he might normally be an energetic kid. After introducing myself to the boy, I felt super sorry for him. "Please bring my brother back. He needs me."

The boy reminded me of the child from the movie "The Sixth Sense." He probably was full of life, but was truly traumatized by having his brother taken.

As we ended the interview, I handed the Aarons my card so they could call me if they heard from the kidnappers. I also assured

them that I would contact them as soon as I had any new
information.

Chapter 7

Andrea Meacham was ready to scream and felt so helpless with Ronald missing. Her panic knew no bounds! He probably had been off his meds since he was taken. Why would someone want to take

him? Just to get back at her husband? Maybe she should have divorced him after the scandal. They had discussed it. Plus there was the fact that he was never around because of his job. Marrying a government worker had been exciting to her once upon a time. Then she had eventually become bitter and resentful over him always being away. He also gave her a hard time for her spending habits. That had led to her getting her own job so she could have her own spending money. After that, having the scandal that had nearly led to his arrest had nearly been the breaking point in their relationship. That event had brought nothing but embarrassment to her. Even her co-workers and management at her grocery store job had begun looking at her differently. Sure, they had not said anything, but their body language indicated that they were uncomfortable around her. There was also the fact that her husband owed money to mob boss, Louie Connelli. Having the mafia angry at your family can certainly lead to sleepless nights. Could he be behind this? That morning, she was trying hard not to think about Ronald. She had to focus on feeding Benjamin. However, he was crying louder than usual. It was hard to give one kid her love when she was frantic about one of her other kids maybe being dead. So far, there had been no ransom demands or any contact from the kidnappers. What did that mean? Benjamin kept crying and she finally lost it.

"Be quiet!" she screamed. "I can't do this anymore!"

"Mom," scolded Brittney, as she ate her breakfast before heading to school.

"Don't talk that way to him. You are his mom!"

Andrea was in complete tears and then directed her anger at Brittney. "I need you to help me out more. I am on the verge of a breakdown!"

"Mom, this is hard for me too!" yelled Brittney. "Ronald is my brother!"

"Well, help me with this brother!" reprimanded Andrea.

"Mom, I'm doing what I can. I have to keep going to school despite what's going on."

"Fine. Just go then. Finish your breakfast and go to school."

Brittney gasped incredulously, finished her breakfast and then stormed out of the kitchen.

***

Brittney absolutely could not focus on the math lesson. She wished the Earth would just open up and swallow her! How could she go on? The *that's her* look she got from her classmates and even some teachers overwhelmed her. Yes, she had been speaking to her compassionate school counselor several times since Ronald had been taken, but there was no escape from this hell! Even the guy that she liked and hoped she might start dating seemed more awkward around her and spoke to her less. The thing was, this crisis of losing her brother helped her understand herself better. She saw herself for what she truly was – a complete snob! The things she always worried about seemed so trivial in light of Ronald being kidnapped. She often fretted about getting a car for her 16th birthday, having the best looking clothes, looking pretty, and looking cool with who she hung out with. She often did not even want to be seen with Ronald at school or even have her friends at her house for what they would think when they saw him. In fact, she often saw Ronald, her own brother, as an inconvenience to her life. She always griped about Ronald going into her room and playing with her stuff. He would chew on her cosmetic items and iPhone. She would then scream at him, but he really did not know better. He was on the functioning level of a two-year old. It wasn't his fault. Supposedly he had not been receiving enough oxygen when her mom, Andrea, was pregnant with him. She truly hoped she would have an opportunity to tell him she loved him and be the supportive sister to him she knew she could and should be.

***

Eleven-year old Kenny VanderPlaats was excited about recess.

He looked forward to the game of tag that he and his friends loved to play. Susan probably would be perched on top of the slide watching the five of them play. Kenny wanted her to like him so she could be his girlfriend someday. He could just imagine them sitting at Taco Bell eating burritos and nachos; oh shoot, he had to stay focused on completing his last work sheet at the independent work station so he would not miss any recess! As he finished his worksheet, Mr. Arnold announced that yellow work was finished. The teacher then had the students line up at the door before going out to play.

After beginning another intense game of tag, Kenny swiftly chased Jonathon gaining on him very quickly. As soon as Kenny caught up with him, Jonathon whirled around and tagged him back.

"Hey, no tag backs!" Kenny announced. "Jonathon is still it!"

Jonathon did not initially chase anyone since he felt Kenny should be it again. However, it quickly became clear that the other kids from the class still expected Jonathon to be it.

After a few more minutes of their game, Kenny wandered to where Susan usually watched from her designated spot. "Hi Susan!" said Kenny.

Man, why can't I think of something more cool to say, thought Kenny. "Will you be my girlfriend?" asked Kenny.

***

"Ok," said Susan.

Kenny's stomach felt such a rush of adrenaline since he believed he now had a girlfriend. He blew her a kiss then ran back to his game of tag with a renewed sense of energy.

Bret Stevens watched through his binoculars as Kenny VanderPlaats continued playing tag at recess. The boy, who had Downs syndrome, had momentarily detoured from his game and talked to some girl who was watching the kids play from the top of a slide. He seemed excited after talking to her. Stevens smiled. Kenny might also be more of a challenge then Adam and Ronald. He seemed rather strong-willed and stubborn at times from what Stevens could tell. Well, he would have to use good teaching practices and management techniques to control Kenny. Stevens inhaled, as he was nervous before every kidnapping. They had done their research; it was now time to execute their plan. He then spoke into his walkie-talkie.

"Are you good to go?" he asked.

"Roger that, Stevens," responded Betty Jones.
"All right, let's move!"

***

Something was not right! I felt a horrible premonition in my gut, as I walked up the front steps of my house in Dairy, Pennsylvania. I had been unwinding at the local bar after a very trying case. In fact, I was also not in much of a hurry to get home. My wife, Sharon, and I had been fighting quite a bit lately. Also, my youngest daughter, Angela, was very good at being 15. If there was a definition of sarcastic, her picture would be by the word in the dictionary or in Google images. She was a good kid, but her teenage hormones and demand for independence were in high gear! Nonetheless, this night, I felt the need to hurry home about mid-way through the drive home. Something just felt off.

As I opened the door, my worst fears became realized. In fact, every spouse's or parent's worst nightmare came true for me! The desk lamp that was an heirloom for Sharon lay scattered all over the living room floor. Her China cabinet had been knocked over and glass was all over the floor. There had clearly been a struggle. And then the blood! Oh, there was blood all over the floor. As I followed its trail, my hands trembled. At the end of the path, I felt like I was sucker punched as I staired down at my very dead wife! I lunged down to her and held her tightly crying uncontrollably. I then began searching through the house and yelling "Angela! Angela!" My real life nightmare continued, as I found her body with a single gunshot wound to the head in the bathroom. "No, no!" I screamed. I wanted so badly to remove my gun from my holster and join my wife and youngest daughter. I had so failed them in not being here for them. However, Aiden and Michelle, who were currently in college, would need me. Plus, my despair did eventually turn to rage. Rage and a promise to eventually find their killer.

Just then the phone rang and awakened me from my recurring nightmare of the night my wife and youngest child were murdered. It was only 10 p.m., and I had fallen asleep in my office.

It was Michelle. "Hi Daddy, you sound stressed. Are you all right?"

"I'm fine. I'm just under a lot of stress with this latest case. Plus, I confronted Jen Noto. She wants to partner up with me to solve this current case. The nerve!"

"Well, my first thought is that you tell her off and keep her away from you, Daddy.
However, maybe she is the kind of person you want to have on your side."

"Come again?" I asked incredulously.

"Well, it's kind of like the old adage. You want to keep your friends close and your enemies closer."

"Ok," I said not totally following my surviving daughter's logic.

"Well, she strikes me as a talented journalist. Perhaps she has resources that might help you."

"But we are the FBI!" I stammered.

"Yeah, but sometimes journalists notice things."

"Huh, that's what she claimed about herself."

"Well, it's up to you, Daddy. Anyway, I think there is something else on your mind. You had another nightmare just now, didn't you?"

"Dang, how do you and so many other women read my mind so well? I'm supposed to be the expert on human psychology!"

"Well, you have taught me much of what you know Pops. Anyway, it has been about seven years since I lost my sister and mom. The anniversary of their deaths is about a month away. This is hard for me too!"

"Yes, Angela really admired you Sweetie! She was studying hard to be a top-notch student like you. She was planning on majoring in pre-law like you were."

"I know. She told me. She also told me that she admired you very much and wanted to be like you when she grew up. She felt such pressure living up to your and my standards."

I closed my eyes as I battled my guilt. I had not been very patient with Angela prior to her death. Her sassiness and attitude had been getting to me. I wish I had been more supportive, compassionate and understanding...heck, I had been going through my own mid-life crisis since I had recently turned 40. Plus, my receding hairline, acid reflux issues and feeling that my body was showing some signs of aging had led me to being more grumpy lately...

"I'm sorry Daddy, I didn't mean to upset you," Michelle said as her own voice began quivering. "I just miss them so much and wish I could have told my sister and Mom how much I loved them..." Just then I noticed that I was getting another call from Bingham. Dang, why did I always have to get calls at such inconvenient times!

"Hon, I've got to go. My boss is calling. I will call you soon."

***

Bobby Vito and Benny Lezza waited with tense anticipation outside the FBI headquarters building. Tonight was the night that they were going to make their move and teach Graham his lesson. When they were done with him, Graham would probably be incapacitated for a very long time, maybe even permanently. One time the two of them had broken a man's legs, and from what they heard, it was years before he fully recovered. There was another man on Connelli's hit list that they had used a baseball bat to hit his back. Again, through the mafia resources, they had learned that he had developed severe spinal trauma and might never completely heal. Yes, that was the price one paid for offending and getting on the bad side of Connelli. That's why most people just let the man be.

"Man, Graham has got to come out some time to go home," said Vito.

"It's like the guy never rests," said Lezza. "Maybe Old Man Connelli has met his match in this Graham. This is the FBI we are talking about. Maybe we should just go home. We've been scoping out this building for three nights!"

Vito then slapped Lezza upside the head. This prick had always been a coward even when they were kids in the old neighborhood. You never crossed and absolutely never disobeyed a direct order from Louie Connelli. The mob boss had principles but was ruthless with people who upset him. Connelli had asked them to teach a lesson to Graham and Vito was determined to follow through with that directive.

"Ow!" stammered Lezza.

"Don't ever suggest we go against Connelli. He was offended when Graham questioned him. He is not afraid of the FBI so we should all be afraid of him!"

"I'm sorry, but the U.S. government is something Connelli is not used to. If he goes after the feds, that could be the end of him. I'm just scared man."

Vito's anger boiled in his stomach like a bloated volcano about to erupt and devour anything in its path. This wuss was only a body guard for Connelli because he was married to Connelli's sister. Lezza always slowed the pair down and this was so frustrating to Vito. Politics truly sucked!

"Oh, here he comes!" said an excited Lezza. "Ok, don't screw this up!" said Vito.

As Graham entered the parking lot, Vito and Lezza jumped out and grabbed a stunned Graham. They quickly duct-taped his mouth and hands.

"Calm down big boy," said Vito in his ears. "We just want to talk. Connelli has a message he wants us to deliver to you." Vito then grabbed a baseball bat from his car and approached Graham. Graham had a look of intemperate fear that Vito had seen many times before maiming Connelli's enemies. He felt no sympathy for this FBI agent.

"Not so fast!" shouted a voice over a bullhorn. "Turn him loose or I'll end both of your lives right now!"

"Who is that?" shouted a frantic Lezza.

Graham felt his life flash before his eyes. This new voice demanding his release sounded super familiar, though. *Oh, my gosh,* he thought, *it's Jen Noto; she is impersonating an FBI agent. My life is in her hands!*

"This is Agent Gates from the FBI."

"Yeah right," shouted Vito, "and I'm the Easter Bunny! We know all the agents went home hours ago. Whoever you are, you'd better turn around and walk away before I..."

"All right then Bobby Vito and Benny Lezza, go ahead and make me pull my
trigger!"

"How do you know our names?" stammered Lezza.

"We are the feds and we have surveillance on everyone! I know your whole history."

"The feds ain't got nothing on me!" shouted a not quite so confident Vito.

"Oh yeah, how do I know about Arthur Middle School where you attended in the inner city of Pennsylvania!" said Noto. "Hey, I'm in a hurry. Leave this agent and never bother him again. If you don't comply, then I'll be forced to shoot your knees and lock your mother, Maria, in a federal prison."

"Hey, leave my mom out of this!" stammered Vito. "You can't arrest her. She is a church-going woman!"

"Hey, we can do anything," snarled the voice. "Tell Connelli you delivered his message, and he won't harm you."

"But if he finds out I lied to him. . ." stammered Vito.

"It is a chance you'll have to take," Noto said. "Maria is depending on it!"

"Ok, let's split man," said Vito.

Lezza needed no prodding as he was already sprinting to the car.

After their car zoomed out, Noto came out from behind the truck she was hiding in and quickly untied a very confused Graham.

"Wow, you always live this much on the edge?" asked Noto, as she freed him and helped him to his feet.

"Hey, what the heck just happened? I recognized your voice, but how did you know what they were doing and all about them?"

"Hey, I told you before, I hear and notice things. I confess, I've been staking out the FBI headquarters building the past several days to gain any access I can to the story. I noticed these two guys that I did not suspect were agents. So I followed them after they got tired of waiting for you after the second night and visited the local bar. They had a lot to drink and ended up reminiscing about old times, their family, etc. They paid me no attention as I listened to their drunken conversation for two hours. Man, I am truly sleep-deprived from following these two goons around but that's the price you pay in my profession. Also, I had done a story on the Connelli family a while back and had visited Augusta, Maine. I had hung out at the local bodega and learned more about the family that way."

"Well, you are quite a resourceful journalist. However, I still can't forgive you for what you did to me."

"I don't blame you. I really can't forgive myself either. Saving you now and helping you find these kids may be my penance. Plus, like I said before, perhaps we can help each other."

"Well, I feel I owe you slightly for saving me from a painful beating tonight, which may have left me permanently maimed. However, if I let you tag along, you must promise to not write anything for the paper until I give you permission. Whatever you learn is strictly off-the-record until I say otherwise!"

"Yes, I totally promise. You will basically be my boss for the duration of this case."

"Thank you. Well, there is some major new news. I'll share it with you since you
saved my neck tonight, but let's go somewhere else other than here. Apparently I'm not safe at the FBI office!"

"You're not going to report what happened here tonight?" asked Noto.

"All my instincts are saying I should, but then you would be indicted for
impersonating an FBI agent."

"You don't think the end would justify the means in this case?"

"I'm not sure, but right now I am more concerned about what I learned tonight.
Let's go to Billy's Pub and I'll tell you about this latest development."

***

At Billy's Pub, I divulged to Noto that there had been a third kidnapping.

"Oh man, there is no way we can keep a lid on this!" she said. "It's going to be all over the papers. I've got to write something!" I was about to berate her for caring more about getting a story, but then she continued, "However, it's more important that you catch whoever is doing this and bring the boys back safely. Do you guys still suspect Connelli?"

"Not really anymore. He has an airtight alibi for the night that Ronald Meacham went missing. Plus, from what I've learned about him, he does care about children. He is a family man and seemed genuinely offended that I was 'accusing' him. I think that's why he wanted to teach me a lesson tonight. I don't think those men were going to kill me."

"Are you afraid they might come back for you?" asked Noto. "I think my ruse fooled and scared them, but you never know."

"Well, right now I feel more of a need to focus on the kidnapping. I think if I stay out of Connelli's hair, I should be safe."

Chapter 8

Gloria Glen enjoyed her job and her life. She had worked for numerous years as a pharmacist at this drug store in the small town of Cedarville, Maine. Her husband was a state trooper and also enjoyed his work. They resided next to a vast forest and sometimes enjoyed hiking in it. There had been a huge factory in the middle of the forest but it had closed down several years ago. Since so many manufacturing jobs were being relocated overseas, this once prosperous business had shut down. Several people in Cedarville had lost their jobs; times were definitely difficult. Gloria got teary-eyed when she thought about what the factory had meant to the town. So far, the factory had not been torn down because of the nostalgic feeling it had as part of this logging down.

Gloria was typing on her computer when a blonde-haired man who had frequented the pharmacy for the past week walked in. "Why hello Mr. North! What can I do for you?"

Tom North again seemed uncomfortable when she spoke to him. Some people were just naturally more private. Again, he asked for a prescription that she knew was usually prescribed to children with special needs. He had said he lived in Brokersville, just a few miles east of Cedarville.

"Now where did you say you worked in Brokersville?" she asked trying to make
conversation as she typed in his information.

"I work at Pete's Pizza," he said looking uncomfortable.

As Gloria filled the order and Mr. North headed on his way, she felt confused. Pete's Pizza had closed down two years ago. Tom North was clearly lying. Why? There was just something off about him. She reminded herself that it was not her business, and she just needed to do her job.

***

After the abduction of Kenny VanderPlaats, FBI

Director Marty Scheelhaase personally attended the next C.A.R.D. team meeting. Now that there were three kidnappings, the media attention for the case gained momentum. Public panic was understandably quite high. There were rumors of parents of special needs students keeping their children home. Local police departments even talked about posting officers at schools since the last two kidnappings occurred at schools. Ventrelli and I sat near the front of the conference table with Noto sitting next to us. A big part of me wanted to have my head examined for allowing Noto to tag along. Was she really sincere about us working together? My past experience told me she had some hidden self-serving agenda.

"What's Ms. TMZ doing here?" asked Jonathon Sparks.

"Hey, she's with me. She and I have an agreement."

"I don't trust her," said Ken Thompson.

"Yeah, me neither. How could you trust this woman after what she did to you?" asked Sparks.

In truth, I was wondering the same thing. Did I dare tell my fellow agents how she had saved me from getting beaten up the previous night? My gut was telling me not to say anything and that this was a time to simply let bygones be bygones.

"Men, trust me. Ms. Noto and I have come to an understanding," I said. "I don't forgive her for what she did to me, but we have kind of a business arrangement."

Ventrelli, Sparks and Thompson all raised their eyebrows in surrender wondering what had gotten into me. I, too, worried that maybe I was losing my touch. My thick- skinned personality had always served me in my career. Was I becoming soft by letting Jen Noto tag along? Heck, I knew I was becoming physically softer. I was only a few years away from the dreaded 50, and my body was showing signs of aging. I became tired much more quickly when playing basketball, my hearing was not as strong as it once was and I noticed aches and pains that I had not noticed before. Heh, some might say this was due to the fact that I had not prayed to God since Sharon and Angela had been murdered. Although I did not believe God acted that way, I also never would have thought he would have taken away my family like he had. Sharon and I had been fairly devout Christians prior to the murders, and we had always been taught to trust in God in good times and bad. However, this situation was way beyond bad and I had given up on being a religious man.

Director Scheelhaase then began the meeting and dispensed with all pleasantries. This case was becoming a national crisis and there was certainly political pressure to get to the bottom of it.

Cutting right to the chase, Scheelhaase said, "I'd like to know what we know so far, what working theories we have and what is being done to return these children. Mr. Graham, you may begin."

I cleared my throat, scratched my forehead and then proceeded with my presentation. "All three of these children come from middle or slightly upper middle class families. The first victim lived with his family in Brooks Valley, Pennsylvania. Ronald Meacham is an 18-year old boy who has what is called severe cognitive impairment. His 15-year old sister walked him outside to watch the train go by their house. At approximately 6 p.m., someone approached the house driving a black SUV and tased the sister and then Ronald vanished. The DMV has not yet found any record of a stolen vehicle matching that description."

I then talked about the various suspects in Ronald's kidnappings and how none of those leads have gotten us anywhere so far. I obviously left out the mysterious hit the night before involving Connelli's two goons.

"The second victim was a 10-year-old child named Adam Aaron from Mapleville, Maine. He has a severe level of autism and was kidnapped while his class was taking a walk on the Birches Elementary School grounds. The kidnapper threw a flash grenade to

64

throw the class into a frenzy. Nobody saw what happened to Adam. His one-on-one or personal assistant teacher had rushed to help rescue another student who had run into the street. We believe that the kidnapper entered and exited the school grounds from a woods directly next to the building. There was a street on the other side of the woods, so it is conceivable that the kidnappers used this route. Unfortunately, no one saw anything. All we have are forensic photographs of the footsteps allegedly used by the kidnapper who carried Adam away.

"The third victim was a boy with Down's syndrome named Kenny VanderPlaats, in Butler, Maine, about 50 miles away from Mapleville, where Aaron was kidnapped. He is 11 and also was just outside the school building when he was snatched. As was done with Adam, the kidnappers threw a flash grenade and used the chaos as an opportunity to snatch Kenny during recess. One child reports seeing a black car drive away, so this is probably the same SUV that was seen fleeing the scene with Ronald Meacham."

I took a deep breath as I poised myself to continue with my presentation.

"So we are obviously dealing with a professional," I said. "All three kidnappings were done very methodically, quickly and without making any serious mistakes. We believe there is probably some military training involved. This case has me very disturbed since the kidnappers are going to so much trouble and obviously spending a ton of money and resources to kidnap these three boys. We've done extensive research into the backgrounds of the families of the boys, but only Ronald's father, Tyler Meacham, has an enemy with a motive and means for enacting revenge. Adam and Kenny's parents have fairly clean backgrounds except for an occasional speeding ticket. So, we have very few leads to go on based on the victims' families. We are currently searching to see if there are any military deserters or personnel who have criminal records. So far the Army, Navy and Air Force have not given us information about deserters. The kidnapper or kidnappers obviously have some fascination with kids with special needs. Since the kidnappings go across state lines, I doubt we are dealing with anyone directly related to their families. What is also noteworthy is that there have been no ransom demands. So the kidnapper obviously does not want money. Which leads me to believe they are being held for personal use."

"Personal use?" one of the agents asked.

"Yes. Perhaps this person or people are emotionally connected to kids with special needs. Possible connections could be that they may have been the parent of a child with special needs. Maybe they had a special needs child who died. Perhaps the perps are curious about children with special needs and want to construct some form of social experiment."

Low murmuring began occurring amongst my colleagues.

"Do you feel that there is a chance the kidnapper is mistreating these children?" asked Noto, which was actually a very good question. Perhaps she wasn't just a sleaze journalist but an inquisitive and thoughtful individual.

"I don't think so," I continued. "Keep in mind that the kidnappers did not use any violence when they conducted the kidnappings. They used a non-lethal taser on the sibling of the first victim and used harmless flash grenades for the next two missions. It is refreshing that the kidnappers have not used violence when conducting the kidnapping, but things could possibly change if the kids resist them or somebody gets in their way. I believe we are dealing with more than one kidnapper since it would have been difficult for one person to get away with each child. More than likely, these people have lots of money. We are currently monitoring to see if there are any cases of people laundering large sums of money."

"We've got to somehow anticipate what child might be next and then capture these creeps!" one agent stammered.

"That narrows it down to about 3 million kids," Sparks sarcastically added.

"So far I have interviewed the families of Ronald Meacham and Adam Aaron. I will be flying out tomorrow to talk to the family of Kenny VanderPlaats. What is also noteworthy is that these kidnappers somehow seem to know exactly when to strike. So ,I believe these three victims were specific targets. These people probably had been watching and researching these three children very closely." I told about the kidnappers knowing about Ronald watching the train, Adam and his class being on their walk and Kenny's class being at recess.

"It's almost like the kidnappers are taking more risks," added Noto. Everyone looked at her. "I mean, the first time, the kidnappers was only dealing with two people, the victim and his sister. The second time, it was just the class. The third time, there were numerous people out at recess so many more potential witnesses. Does that pattern mean anything?"

***

K enny felt anger boil through him, as he and these two other boys were escorted into what looked like a classroom. This was not his school, and these people were not his family. After he had been grabbed after the explosion at his school, someone had grabbed him and stuck a needle in him. When he woke up, he felt very scared but then fairly calm. Now he felt angry again!

The man that had greeted him in his strange bed this morning led the three of them into this classroom. There was another man in the corner who was much younger than the man who had woken him. Then a woman, who also looked young, walked in. She was dressed like an army lady.

"Ok boys," said the man who had brought them to this room. "Find a desk that has your name on it."

Just then the older boy began wandering toward a rug in the corner of the room and began chewing on a toy.

The first man walked over to him and said, "Now Ronald, it is time to sit in your desk. You may hold onto this toy."

After the three of them were sitting in desks, the man began speaking while standing next to the dry erase board at the front of the room.

"Welcome boys, my name is Mr. Stevens and I will be your teacher."

"Teacher, Mrs. Smith," said the red-headed boy whom Kenny thought was about his age.

"Now Adam, it is Mr. Steven's turn to speak."

Mr. Stevens then walked to what looked like a classroom schedule similar to what Kenny had seen in his school. "First we will do calendar, then you may have a snack. Then we will do math and then centers."

Mr. Stevens then went through the rest of the schedule.

"Now, there are three teachers in this classroom. I am Mr. Stevens," he said pointing to his name on the board. "This is Mr. Penders."

Penders had wavy hair and wore all black. He waived his hand to them but did not look very friendly. Kenny shuddered.

"And this is Ms. Jones." Jones also raised her hand but also looked mean.

"We are all your teachers and you need to do what we say. Here are the rules. When you follow the rules, you will be on level 1. When you are on level 1, you may do one of your favorite activities. Ronald, you may use the vacuum toy I have. Adam, you may play on the computer and Kenny, you can play Wii-U. If you are bad, you need to sit in the cooldown area."

He then pointed to a big piece of paper that said "rules" on top. "Rule number one, listen to your teachers. Rule number two, use kind words. Rule number three, be kind to classmates."

"When school is done, you will go back to your rooms and do chores. When chores are done, you may have play time. We have video games, a basketball court, and a playground area. Then we will have dinner, and then you boys will have homework. Then you guys may have quiet times in your rooms."

Despite the fact that Mr. Stevens seemed like a kind teacher, Kenny's anger overwhelmed him. "When do I get to see mom and dad?" he bellowed.

Mr. Stevens actually looked kind of sad but said, "Boys, you won't be seeing your parents for a while. You will be staying here for a while, but you will eventually see your parents."

"Yeah right," murmured the lady named Ms. Jones.

Mr. Stevens then gave her an angry look.

"No, this is not my school! This is not my home. I. Want. To. Go. Home! I hate
you!" shouted Kenny.

"Kenny VanderPlaats!" scolded Mr. Stevens. "That is not using kind words. I know this is a big change, but you must be a good boy."

"No, I am not staying! Get away from me!"

"Kenny, you are now down to level two," said Stevens while moving Kenny's name from the level one section on the board to the level two area.

Ronald then jumped up from his seat and threw his toy after he had chewed it thoroughly. He stood up and began walking toward the play area. Adam also became anxious and jumped up from his seat, leaving the Kusch ball that had been keeping him calm. He jumped up and began running in circles.

Kenny then ran toward the door and began kicking it savagely.

While Mr. Stevens and Mr. Penders tried hard to get the three of them back in their seats, Ms. Jones walked into the closet and brought out what looked like an electric razor. She walked up to Kenny and shocked him. "Ow!" screamed Kenny. The energy drained from him and he fell to the floor in more pain then he had ever been in. He cried and screamed like he never had before!

"No Betty!" shouted Mr. Stevens. "That is not how we do things here."

She ignored him and went and zapped Ronald who screamed and passed out. Mr. Penders was able to calm Adam down before he suffered a similar fate.

A furious Stevens now shouted at Betty Jones. "That is not how I run my classroom! We use non-violent methods to control these kids! If that happens again, you are fired!"

"So fire me!" remarked Jones. "Who else is going to help you maintain order here?"

Mr. Stevens, who was still red in the face, stood frozen but said nothing.

"Think about it," continued Jones. "You can't kidnap these kids and keep them here forever and expect them to behave. They've lost everything! When you hired Penders and me for this mission, you knew you were making an immoral choice. If you want to follow this plan through, you've got to be tough and use extreme measures to show them you're in charge. I appreciate what you're paying me, but you need to follow my lead once in a while. I was in the army and know how to demand compliance!"

"You can't use a taser on these kids!" stammered Stevens. "It could really hurt them or even kill them!"

An unfazed and emotionless Jones said, "I am using a very non-lethal taser. This is a TF-76."

Stevens still looked at her with terror and revulsion.

"Trust me, this kind of taser was only designed to cause minimal pain and not cause loss of muscle control. I have other tasers I could use if these boys become more out of control."

"Fine, use your methods once in a while. However, first let me do things my way. If I decide that extreme measures are necessary, I will authorize you to use your methods."

"Yes sir," said a sarcastic Jones.

Kenny shook uncontrollably fearing that he might be having one of his seizures. Kenny briefly made eye contact with Adam and then passed out.

Chapter 9

s I ate my cheesy potato burrito while on my way home, my thoughts drifted to Sharon's case. It had been officially unsolved, and this bothered me. I had not been officially part of the investigation since that would have been a conflict of interest. Agent Ken Thompson had been the lead agent and had done what he could. He had followed up on my wife's patient, Armon Luck, whom my wife had written about in her diary. Noto, who had claimed to have been a family member of Sharon's, had asked to go through her belongings. She had then found the diary, read about my wife secretly meeting Armon Luck, and had suggested in the newspaper article that they had been having an affair. The headline read **"Murdered FBI Agent's Wife Cheating With Mental Patient?"** I had been furious at Jen Noto and sued her. The case went nowhere, though, and I had never completely forgiven her. A part of me still wondered why I was letting her work with me on this current kidnapping case and even befriending her. However, she had saved me from an ugly beating a day ago at the hands of Connelli's goons.

Anyway, Armon Luck had been interviewed by the police and FBI but had been allegedly in his room at the hospital when she was murdered. His nurse, Anne Potocki, had claimed that Armon Luck had been in his room between 8 and 10 p.m. and Sharon's time of death had been 8:30. With no evidence whatsoever linking Luck to the crime scene, the case went cold. Things had gotten dicey when Thompson had asked to see the records of what my wife had wanted to talk to him about. The whole doctor-patient privacy privilege! Thompson had tried to get a subpoena for the therapy sessions between Sharon and Luck. He had argued about the fact that Armon Luck did have a history of battery against women and sexual assault. However, the judge needed more evidence to authorize a subpoena of the files. So, the case went nowhere, and Armon Luck still resided at the psychiatric hospital. If he had indeed murdered Sharon and Angela, mental illness or not, he needed to pay!

***

Adam Aaron ate his food and tried not to cry. He missed his mom, dad and brother. Why was he here? The two other boys sat on each side of him. The one boy with the glasses was cutting up his food and also seemed angry. The tall boy on the other side seemed like he didn't care but was just happy to be eating. The man who called himself the teacher sat at the head of the table and kept showing him pictures of what was coming next in the day. Therefore, Adam felt a little bit better but still wanted his family back. The mean woman stood guard by the door of the room, and the other man was sitting off to the side playing on his phone. Adam loved playing on his dad's phone and any computer. As a young child, he had often deleted programs or files without knowing how he had done it. The world of computers made more sense to him than the regular world where everybody kept talking all the time. People talking too much always stressed him out and made him mad.

After they had finished, Mr. Stevens showed the boys the picture strip and said
"Ok guys, dinner is all done, it is time for play time."

"No, it is time to go home!" shouted the boy with the glasses.

The mean-looking man and the woman seemed ready to rush over and restrain him as they had the other day. However, Mr. Stevens said, "Kenny, I know you are upset. You will see your parents soon. Now it is time to go play your favorite games and have fun!"

Kenny seemed ready to fight more but then seemed to think better of it. As the three boys were taken to the giant playroom, Adam felt much better. There were a whole bunch of computers for him to play with! There was a basketball hoop, video arcade games,

73

and even a small playground. The tall boy named Ronald began swinging on one of the swings in the playground, and Kenny rushed to a pinball machine. As Adam began accessing the all programs menu on the nearest computer to see what games they had, Mr. Penders quickly pulled up a chair beside him.

"Not so fast Rain Man!" said Penders. "You can't be on the computer by yourself. I have to be watching you at all times. Not like you can contact anyone on the outside anyway. This network is completely hacker proof, so don't get any ideas."

Chapter 10

Andrea walked down the stairs after another mostly sleepless night. Thank God Tyler had decided to take time off of his job and step up to help with Benjamin. Otherwise, she did not know how or if she would make it. So many people these last few days had offered well-intended advice such as "Ronald will be found soon, I'm sure he's fine," etc. However, there was really no describing what she was going through. These last few days had been like the worst Hell imaginable. Andrea could not imagine Hell being much worse. Knowing your child had been kidnapped and was completely helpless anyway was horrible! As she reached the bottom of the stairwell, she noticed a light on in the kitchen. That was strange. Could somebody be in her house? Right now, if there was an intruder in her house, she did not really care what happened to her. However, if something else happened to one of the other members of the family; no, she would not allow anything to happen to another family member! So, she grabbed a candlestick and cautiously approached the kitchen. As she stepped into the kitchen with the candlestick in position to swing if necessary, she nearly screamed. Her daughter, Brittney, was at the kitchen table reading.

"Mom, what the heck are you doing?"

"Right now, wondering the same thing about you."

"Sorry Mom, I am down here because I just can't sleep."

"I can't sleep either. These last few days have been horrible."

"Mom, where can he be? I miss him so much!"

"I don't know! I am worried sick and don't know how I can go on if something bad happened to him."

"As much as I often thought of him as a pain, I really miss him. I miss him chewing on my iPod, almost drinking my shampoo, and drooling all over my scrapbooks. I'd give anything to have my brother back! I actually feel very, very guilty. I hate myself right now!"

"Sweetheart, why do you hate yourself? Talk to me."

"I don't know. You might hate me if I tell you about a thought I had the other day."

"Brittney, you are my daughter, and I love you. We all have fleeting thoughts that we regret. Please tell me. We have to talk to each other and be there for each other."

When Brittney didn't respond, Tyler walked into the room in his bathrobe.

"Your mom is right, Brittney," he said. "We do have to stick together and be honest with each other. I know that sounds strange coming from me since I screwed up royally gambling and then using state funds to pay off my debts. I brought shame to you two and actually placed both of you in danger. I will never really forgive myself. However, all I can do is try to be the best husband and father from here on out. Whatever you thought can't be as bad as what I did. However, if you don't want to tell us, that is fine too."

Brittney exhaled. "I guess I should let it out. You know, my life has been very difficult having Ronald as a brother. I often worry about not living the life that I want. Since a young age, I figured that I would probably have to take care of Ronald when he is an adult. Therefore, I wouldn't be able to use my money for myself."

"Honey, I think it's completely normal to feel that way when you have a brother like Ronald."

"Yeah, but the other day, I actually got a rush of adrenaline and relief when contemplating not having to worry about him anymore. Being able to live my own, self- centered, self-indulged materialistic life!" She paused and looked at the floor. "That thought passed and then I felt guilt like I never had experienced before. Ugh! I hate myself!"

Andrea and Tyler both embraced their 15-year old daughter.

"You have always been a great sister for him," said Andrea. "I don't tell you that enough, but you've always looked out for him.

Even though you are a younger sister, you have always taken care of him."

"Just not when someone kidnapped him the other day."

"Don't you dare blame yourself!" exclaimed Tyler. "Someone else took Ronald, and the FBI and police are looking everywhere for him. These people were professionals who took him and they knew what they were doing."

Andrea became reflective again, as she thought about her firstborn child. As tears began seeping out of her eyes, she began, "I remember the look in his brown eyes after the doctor pulled him from my stomach. At that moment, I truly learned what love was. Even after the doctors labeled him as developmentally delayed since he wasn't crawling or sitting up on schedule, I never loved him any less. He always has been and always will be my baby just like you and Benjamin."

"Mom, you are going to make me start crying now!"

"As am I," said Tyler with a tear beginning to drip down his face.

"We haven't had a heart-to-heart like this in a long time. Life has been hectic and busy," said Andrea.

"Yeah, unfortunately it has taken a tragedy like this to help at least me realize what is really important in life. I feel like such a snob always worrying about having all the cool things, fitting in with the right crowd, having a boyfriend. This has made me completely rethink my priorities. I just hope the cost is not losing my brother."

"I hope not either," said Andrea as tears began cascading out of her eyes again. "I love you Brittney!"

"I love you, too, Mom!"

"We can all get through this together," said Tyler. "Now let's all try to get to sleep so we can somewhat function for the rest of the day. We want to be ready in case Ronald returns tomorrow!"

As they began to head back upstairs, Andrea added "I just hope they are taking good care of Ronald. Hopefully someone is giving him his medication. I sure hope there is a woman taking care of him. No offense, Tyler."

"Hey, none taken!"

Brittney froze.

"What's going on Brittney? Did I say something?" asked Andrea.

"Mom, you are a genius! That's it!"

"What's it?" said a befuddled and confused Andrea.

Brittney continued to marvel in her revelation. "When the FBI guy interviewed me, I told him there was something strange about the kidnapper. I now know what it was because of you! The person who grabbed and shoved Ronald into the black SUV was a woman!"

***

I flew on the FBI jet out to Butler, Maine, to meet with the

VanderPlaats. Brittney Meacham had called my direct extension in the middle of the previous night and informed me that the kidnapper had been a woman.

Even though she had a ski mask on, Brittney could tell from her figure that it was a female. This could be a valuable clue to add to the profile of the kidnappers. After exiting the jet, I met with the Butler detective liaison, Beth Holmes, and drove to the home of Kenny's mom. We were greeted by Angela and Gary VanderPlaats. Mrs. VanderPlaats had a one-year old daughter in the other room.

"I don't know why we have to answer the same questions again," said Mr. VanderPlaats. "We have already met with Ms. Holmes and an agent from the local field office."

"I am the head of the C.A.R.D. team," I explained. "I try to interview everyone involved in the case to keep information centralized. Plus, when you get asked the same questions several times, you might remember extra information."

Mrs. VanderPlaats seemed ok with this, but Mr. VanderPlaats still seemed skeptical.

After asking many of the same questions, I got many of the same answers. No one had really seen anything of value. Kenny had no real enemies. In fact, Mrs. VanderPlaats explained that Kenny "always brought a smile to the face of strangers and was incredibly kind and empathetic." The only problem was that Kenny had experienced some bullying at his school. I grimaced at how unfair life could be at times. It is a travesty that sometimes those who are the kindest often get taken advantage of and bullied the most. Heck, that was one of the reasons I became a police officer and then an FBI agent – to protect the innocent from the bad guys.

"The biggest lie told in schools," said Mrs. VanderPlaats, "is that schools don't tolerate bullying. Bullying is very much tolerated, and schools often do very little to stop it. Whenever the school tried to include Kenny in the general education classroom, a few kids always began picking on him. So, I demanded that he be put back in the self- contained classroom."

"I still feel like you are having him run away from his problems by removing him from those classes," said Gary VanderPlaats.

"Gary, not now! Plus, I don't think Kenny has a fair chance of being able to stand
up for himself against bullies."

"He doesn't, because you baby him! If he spent more time at my house, I could teach him to stand up for himself!"

I had a feeling at the beginning of the conversation that I was dealing with a divorced couple. Their body language and personal proximity habits matched the description of such a couple, but it was hard to be sure.

"Gary, stop it!" she yelled.

"Folks, this isn't helping," I said.

She settled down and continued about Kenny. "He perseveres at everything he does, and it is always a joy to celebrate with him after he accomplishes a task. He does tend to be a bit stubborn at times, though. I hope whoever has him doesn't get frustrated and hurt him!" Angela VanderPlaats paused, and her lips quivered. "Why?" she wailed. "Why did somebody take my baby?"

Although I am sure that was a rhetorical question, I explained my theory with her that I had with the Meachams and Aarons to put her mind at ease. After going over a few more things with them including setting up the bugging device on the phone, Holmes and I left.

***

The next morning, Holmes and I visited the school where Kenny had disappeared. We analyzed the ingress and egress the kidnappers had apparently taken. Mr. Jensen, the principal, showed us the wood chip playground where Kenny had been playing at recess. The kidnapper or kidnappers had entered and exited through the perimeter fence surrounding the school. As had been done at the other two kidnapping sites, no fingerprints had been left. These guys were clearly pros. What was also strange was that the perimeter door to the fence had a computerized locking system. Most schools in our post 9/11, post Columbine and Sandy Hook school shooting era, had similar security systems.

"How did they breach the security system? Did somebody let them in?" I asked.

"No," said Mr. Jensen. "The initial detectives asked the same question. All of the staff on duty did not see a thing. The kidnappers were already in the gate."

I nodded as I gathered my thoughts. "So they parked out here, somehow breached the computerized locked door, entered the playground wearing ski-masks, threw a flash grenade and made off with Kenny."

"That sums it up!" said the principal who then began to get choked up. "Please find him. He was such a wonderful kid. Kenny had the biggest heart of any kid in our school. He loved drawing, making things with his hands and gave hugs to pretty much everyone he knew. He was actually quite a caregiver for the other kids. He loved pushing kids in wheelchairs, carrying books for kids..." He sniffled and struggling to compose himself. "Why would some professional kidnappers just take him?" he said on the verge of completely breaking down. "I'm sorry."

Holmes handed him a clean handkerchief, and I said, "It's all right, we all need to express our emotions at times."

Truth was, I was pretty worried myself. Why would professional kidnappers go to this much trouble for these kids? These kidnappers were using hacking and computer expertise, military supplies and superior stealth to make their snatches. This case was by far the most bizarre I had ever been a part of and I had seen some strange ones.

Next, we interviewed the student who had witnessed the black SUV driving off, but got very little extra information from what we already knew.

After that, Holmes and I studied the photos that the local forensics team had taken of the footprints left by the kidnappers. Since the ground had been wet from rain, we got a clearer view of the footsteps.

"There is something about these footprints," I said.

"What's that?" asked Holmes. "Are they not human feet? Sheesh, I can't imagine a human doing what these kidnappers are doing."

"No, it's something else," I said. "I think these are the feet of a woman."

Chapter 11

After I returned home from Butler, Maine, I met with the C.A.R.D. team and with several of the FBI analysts. We accessed our files and searched specifically for women in our VICAP database. I also reached out to my contact at the Pentagon to see if there were any deserters from the armed services who were women. It was quite obvious that the kidnappings of Ronald, Adam and Kenny had been done by a female as evidenced by the footprints we had analyzed at Adam and Kenny's school and Brittney Meacham's eyewitness account of Ronald's abduction. Afterwards, I met with Jen Noto at a back table at T.G.I. Friday's to update her about the case and other stuff that had been on my mind lately. Maybe I was clearly sleep deprived, but I chose to bring up my wife's case to Noto. If we were going to work together, perhaps it was time to let the elephant out of the bag.

"You still don't trust me!" said Noto.

"Can you blame me?" I asked incredulously.

"No, not at all," said Noto.

"I can't get your article out of my head."

"Sometimes my sleaze journalist talents are what got me to where I am. My nose for a good story gets people hooked, and I always run with it no matter who gets hurt."

"Yeah, your story got me hooked, and what you said in it still haunts me. I think
that is why I have hated you for so long."

"You don't think your wife was having an affair? Deep down, I have always known I was wrong for suggesting something so horrible."

"No, it's not that I think she was having an affair. I'm still curious as to why she wanted to meet with Armon Luck. Her murder was never solved and I was not allowed to go near the case because of the conflict of interest."

"Did you ever suspect something was off with your wife?" asked Noto.

"I think so. She seemed preoccupied in the final days of her life."

"So the case went cold, and her homicide was never solved?"

"Correct. They suspected her neediest patient, Armon Luck, but agents Ken Thompson and Jonathon Sparks discovered that he had an alibi on the night Sharon and my daughter were murdered."

"I wasn't able to find out the other details of the story," said Noto. "Who was Luck's alibi?"

"His nurse was. Anne Potocki claimed she administered his medications during the time he was in his room. Wait a minute, why am I telling you this? Are you going to write a story?"

"Mark, the story is hardly newsworthy, unless we find new evidence. Ok, I promise that whatever you tell me about your wife's cold case will be strictly off the record."

Maybe I was a sucker, but she did seem truly sincere and remorseful about her past actions. "Ok, Anne Potocki administered his medications twice between the times of eight and ten. My wife's TOD – Time of Death – was believed to be in that time period."

"Maybe I'm going crazy," said Noto, "but I'd like to talk to the staff from the hospital."

"Sorry?" I asked.

"I would like to speak with this Anne Potocki and any other staff from this state hospital."

"Whoa, are you crazy?" I asked.

"Look, I'm feeling very guilty about spreading gossip about your wife's intentions in that story all those years ago. I feel that in a roundabout way that helping to shed light on your wife's case is like my penance."

"I trust that you are remorseful, but this is crazy! I could lose my job agreeing to have you impersonate an FBI agent..."

"Mark, I don't have to impersonate an FBI agent, I can just go as a concerned former relative. I had a double major in theater in college, that's why I am such a good actress. That's how I was able to fool those mobsters into thinking I was an FBI agent."

"The answer is no. If something happens to you, I'll have my family's death and your being busted or killed hanging over my head! Let's just focus on finding Ronald,

Adam and Kenny."

"Mark, I am a big girl and can take care of myself. I take full responsibility for whatever happens. I'm doing this with or without your permission, but I'd feel better about it if I had your blessing."

"You are a strange and complicated woman!" I said in an exasperated tone.

"Just give me your blessing to go to the hospital once or twice. If you're not satisfied with whatever I find after two visits, I will stop investigating. Deal?"

"I guess," I said feeling that I was probably being manipulated. "Obviously whatever you find is 100% off the record."

"Obviously," said Noto.

"Just one more thing," I said. "Let agent Ken Thompson go with you. He is a veteran agent and I trust his instincts. He won't go with you as an FBI agent, but he'll be working undercover."

"I suppose I'd better let him go with me. That's a small price to pay."

***

Betty Jones snickered as she watched Bret Stevens playing a game with the two younger boys, Adam and Kenny. He was using one of his teaching methods to help them with turn taking during playing games. Stevens had some visual tool that on one side said "My turn" and on the other side "You're turn." It was to help them with the social skills of playing games. Kenny, the boy with Down's syndrome, had tried to control the game, but Stevens kept referring to the visual tool. Adam hummed quite a bit and needed redirecting but overall stayed focused on the game. Why was Stevens trying to prepare them for adulthood? This wussy man had such an obsessive need for being a teacher, and had gone to such an extreme measure by hiring Penders and Jones, who felt nothing for these kids. She was in this only for the money. She had to get her money from Stevens, and then she would probably kill him, the boys and possibly, Penders. There was no way she could leave witnesses. They had all seen her face. She rarely ever left any witnesses for the various mercenary crimes she committed. She already had an extensive off-shore account in another name. However, she loved the thrill of controlling others and making money in doing so.

***

As Jen Noto and Ken Thompson pulled into the hospital where Armon Luck was still a patient, Noto felt strange. She was used to going on undercover and risky assignments; that was why she had become a journalist. However, this was different. She was not chasing a story; she was simply after the truth – the truth of what happened to FBI agent Mark Graham's wife and daughter. Although as a journalist she had been concerned about the truth despite her questionable tactics, this was unchartered territory for her. She had rarely if ever risked her own well-being to help another human being.

"Tell me again why you think it is a good idea to arrive after visiting hours and without calling?" agent Ken Thompson asked Noto.

"As a reporter, I feel that I always get my best stories when I have the element of surprise. If we call in advance, they may suspect something suspicious."

"But we are not looking for a story," said Thompson.

"I know that. But I still feel that I would have the upper hand in this 'investigation' if I have the element of surprise."

"You honestly think we are going to get any information from anyone let alone a chance to 'visit' Luck when we are arriving after visiting hours and without calling in advance?"

"Leave that to me," said Noto. "I am pretty good at talking my way into about anything." Noto approached the front desk.

The middle-aged desk receptionist eyed her with a bored expression. "May I help
you?"

"Yes," said Noto. "I am here to visit Armon Luck. I am his sister and have not seen him in a long time."

"Visiting hours ended an hour ago, miss. You will have to come back tomorrow."

"Ma'am, my boyfriend here and I have traveled for two days; can we just have five minutes with him?"

"You may, tomorrow from 10 a.m. and 2 p.m." said the 60ish looking lady with thick glasses.

"But I will have to travel back home tomorrow!" said Noto increasing the panicked expression in her voice. "I have a job that will require me to travel home super quickly, and I then may have to go another two years before I see my brother again!"

"Then you probably should have come earlier or called to set up an appointment," said the lady sounding like a teacher scolding a belligerent student.

"Come on honey," said Thompson, who eyed her with an 'I told you so' look.

Noto gestured for Thompson to wait just a moment. "Ma'am, please," she said in a pleading voice. "I miss my brother so much, and if I stay tomorrow and miss another day of work, I will get fired." Before the annoyed-looking receptionist could make a counter argument, Noto continued, "My ex-husband has not paid alimony in months! If I lose my job, the state will take my kid. My douchebag ex-husband wants to do this to punish me for leaving him!"

The receptionist had relaxed features but still did not look ready to give in. "I am sorry for your troubles miss but..."

"The court has sided with him, and he got the house!"

"What! The darn justice system!"

"Yes, he has abused my son and me emotionally and physically, and this is just one more way he can hurt me by not paying alimony and making me lose my baby!"

"What a scum!" exclaimed the receptionist.

"I miss my brother so much, so please just let us see him! I am sorry I did not get here during visiting hours. What's more, my ex always made fun of Armon Luck, and he does whatever he can to hurt me–"

"It's ok miss, let me call the floor and you can spend a few minutes seeing your brother and talking to the nurse."

Thompson mouth hung wide open in astonishment as Noto took his arm and escorted him to the waiting area. After they were out of ear shot from the receptionist, Thompson whispered to her "That was a pretty impressive performance Jennifer Lawrence! Do you use that ruse every time?"

"No, not really. I always analyze my environment and use whatever clues I can use as leverage. In this case, I noticed that the woman had the imprint of a wedding ring on her ring finger. Therefore, I deduced that she was a divorced woman. Plus, her gray hair and wrinkles further led me to believe that she had had a bad experience with men. Her bitter and tough exterior were further signs that she was a woman who has had to overcome male dominance in her life. So I used my fictitious experience to make a connection with her."

"Nice!" remarked a flabbergasted Ken Thompson.

Just then a nurse walked through the locked door and approached them. "I am Armon Luck's nurse, Anne Potocki. Please come with me."

Noto tried hard to hide her excitement at talking to the very nurse who had provided the alibi for Luck. So she continued with the front.

Potocki escorted them to a guest lounge room and they sat on the couch to talk about Luck before seeing him.

"So you are Luck's brother?" asked a confused and suspicious Potocki. "I thought he only had two brothers."

"Well, my parents and I are not exactly on speaking terms so they probably did not mention me."

"I see," said a still doubtful looking Potocki.

"How is my brother doing?" asked Noto wanting to change the direction of this conversation.

"Before we go to see him, I want to forewarn you that today has been a rough day for him."

"That's fine," said Noto. "I am used to his paranoid delusions and mental issues. I know how to talk to him in those instances. How is he doing in general?"

"I can only tell you so much considering the patient/client privilege laws," said Potocki. "He is very needy and has regressed. His paranoid delusions have increased in frequency and duration lately. He believes the government is out to get him."

"Yeah, those episodes started for him at a young age," said Noto trying to be careful not to divulge anything too specific in case there was a discrepancy in what actually happened at a young age.

"Yes, and his delusions of grandeur continue, as he believes very strongly that he is God's gift to women. He continues to flirt with me and every nurse in the ward. We have increased his medications, but his violent acting out continues to be a problem."

"So, does he mainly attack women when they don't flirt back or return his affection?" asked Thompson.

"Yes, so we will probably need to change his medication," said Potocki.

"What about the bizarre murder charges he received involving that woman and her teenage daughter a while ago?" said Noto.

"What about it?" asked Potocki, whom Noto noticed tensed up considerably.

"We were all distressed when we heard back home about him being accused of murder. I know he has his problems and his mental illness, but I don't think he would ever kill anyone," said Noto.

"I know he couldn't have killed that woman," said Potocki who still seemed shaky. "He was in his bed during that time and it was during my shift. I administered his meds at 8 o'clock and 10:30."

"And there was no way he could have slipped out between that time?" asked Thompson, who received a disapproving look from Noto.

"I thought you believed in his innocence," said a confused Potocki.

"I do," said Thompson. "I just like playing devil's advocate to do away with any and all doubt."

"Can my boyfriend and I see him alone please?" asked Noto. Potocki tensed up more.

"That is highly irregular. By hospital policy, I am required to stay with you in his room..."

"I just feel that he will be more comfortable and willing to open up to me if it is just Judd and me," said Noto gesturing toward Thompson. "If you are there, he will be flirting with you and put up a macho façade in front us. He and I had a special bond as kids and I am one of the few people he trusts."

Potocki sighed and shrugged. "I see where you are coming from. I will give you five minutes but no more since that will risk me getting in trouble."

Thompson eyed Noto with an even greater level of respect for her ability to talk her way into anything.

***

As Potocki escorted Noto and Thompson to the room of this man who had potentially murdered Graham's wife and daughter, Noto's stomach was in knots. She truly was crazy for doing this! Although she had a physically imposing FBI agent with her, being in the same room with this mentally ill patient who not only may have been a murderer but also a serial womanizer and rapist scared the crap out of her. Maybe her depression had given her a subconscious suicidal attitude.

As she and Thompson hastily approached the room of Armon Luck, she felt like she was in one of those movies where the audience yell at the screen and say "Don't go in that room!"
As they entered, she was actually relieved to see that Luck was sleeping.

"Great, he's sleeping!" said Thompson. "Now what? What are you thinking? We
should not even be here!"

"I think we're ok," said Noto trying to put herself at ease as much as Thompson. "My gut is telling me that this Potocki woman is somehow turning off the security cameras that lead to the room."

"So what now?" asked Thompson again.

"Let's play detectives," said Noto. "You are an FBI agent, aren't you? Let's look around the room to see if we find anything noteworthy."

90

As they looked around the mildly furnished room, they were about to give up when Ken Thompson eyed Noto as if he had seen a ghost. "I found something, and I think we should go right now!"

"I agree!" said Noto. "I think Luck is about to wake up, and our luck – no pun intended – is about to run out. Let's go!"

As they booked out of the room, they thanked Potocki and went on their way.

***

I sat with Noto, Thompson and Jonathon Sparks at a Buffalo Wild Wings as they claimed they had urgent news to share about my wife and daughter's cold case. It felt weird that I was allowing them to pursue this side mystery unofficially when we had to find the three missing boys. I could probably be subject to disciplinary action allowing this to happen when we could be losing valuable time and resources in finding Adam, Ronald and Kenny. Nonetheless, my curiosity won out this evening as I asked Noto and Thompson to share their findings.

Noto first explained about how in the initial file, Thompson had reported that Potocki had explained that she had administered the medication and checked on Armon Luck at 8 and 10 p.m.

"When we talked to her today," said Noto. "She claimed that she had given him his meds at 8:00 and 10:30."

"So there is obviously a discrepancy in her story," said Agent Sparks with a reflective look in his eyes.

"That may not mean anything," I said. "She may just have forgotten that detail. Even so, it would have been impossible for Luck to have murdered my wife and daughter at 9 p.m."

"Well, call it a woman's intuition if you want, but I sensed an obvious difference in Potocki when we began asking her questions about the night of the murder. Her perspiration went up and she became noticeably more nervous."

"Which suggests that she may have been lying or hiding something," I said. Noto seemed fairly knowledgeable about behavioral analysis, which had often been my specialty. I guess that skill served her well when interviewing for a story.

"There is more," said Thompson. "When we searched around the room, there was a hutch credenza. I peeked behind it not wanting to leave any stone unturned and noticed a secret passageway!"

That got all of our attention.

"That is indeed very disturbing," said Sparks. "So it would have been possible for Luck to have snuck out of the facility without security noticing."

"Yes, and it does seem plausible that this nurse, Ms. Potocki, was and is probably trying to hide something," I stated.

"Could Ms. Potocki be trying to protect Armon Luck?" Noto asked.

"Well, he supposedly flirted with all the women on the floor," said Sparks. "I suppose Ms. Potocki decided she had feelings for him and was seduced into disabling the security cameras. It won't be the first time a patient has manipulated a doctor or a nurse."

"So what do we do now?" said Thompson. "This rogue case is very risky."

"I think we have to talk to Ms. Potocki again," said Noto. "Since she is trying to hide something, we need to figure out what. We also need to figure out why your wife, Sharon, wanted to meet secretly with Luck."

"Not now," I said. "We have to continue to try and find the boys. Jen, I can't have my agents continuing to baby sit you on this crazy expedition."

"Mark, I am a big girl–"

"I know you are," I said. "But this is crazy and could affect your job, my job, Ken and everybody else's job. This could blow up into being a huge scandal. Let's lie low for a while and then we can pursue this at a later time."

***

Jen Noto, Ventrelli, Bingham, Sparks, Thompson and a few other agents and I sat in a conference room at the FBI headquarters building and went over the kidnapping case for a full debriefing.

As head of the C.A.R.D. team, I got right down to the point. "So we have three kidnappings involving special needs children. Two of the children are from upper-middle class homes. The VanderPlaats are from a slightly lower middle-class town. Two of them are from Maine but the other is from Pennsylvania. Two of them were taken while in school while the first was abducted while at home. So, the only real commonality is that they have special needs. The kidnapper or at least one of them is probably a female. Brittney Meacham thought the kidnapper looked like it might have been a female. I am certain that the photos taken at Kenny's school show the footprints of a female."

I then reviewed with them the file prepared by our team of computer technicians who had accessed the database of possible people fitting various kidnapper profiles. Since the kidnapper or kidnappers apparently had military training, we first looked at the reviews of AWOL soldiers since the army had finally provided some of the files.

Only two of the AWOL soldiers seemed to remotely have a chance of being our perps. An Alan Anderson from Maryland had deserted the army five years ago. However, nothing in his background seemed to suggest why he might have a need to start kidnapping kids. A Bob Peeler from Vermont had been AWOL for three years and had a younger brother with Down's syndrome.

Peeler did have some petty theft in his background but nothing to suggest why he might have snapped and began kidnapping other kids like his brother.

We looked at the file for a Susan Eigenheer who was in our VICAP file. She had done time for murdering the man whom she blamed for making her son an invalid.

"She definitely has a connection to kids with special needs," Sparks said. "It is obvious that the drunk driver who hit her son caused the child to have traumatic brain injury, thus causing him to have mentally retardation for the rest of his life."

"Heck, I'd probably want to have revenge on someone if they ruined my child's life like that," another agent said.

"True, but what would she have to gain by kidnapping kids with special needs?" asked Noto. A few of the agents eyed her with annoyance, not knowing why this reporter was being given such close proximity to the case. In some ways, I still could not believe I had let her tag along.

"Well, we need to question her," I said. I then assigned two of the agents to fly out to her home in Illinois and question her. "What about the Gorskis from Plainesville, Ohio? They had a child with Down's syndrome who was left on a school bus and then died. Mr. Gorski then was sent to prison for shooting the negligent bus driver."

"Yes, but again I don't see what motive he would have for kidnapping our three missing boys," said Sparks thoughtfully. "Plus, their socioeconomic status does not fit our profile of the kidnapper having lots of money."

I nodded feeling the frustration of facing dead end after dead end. So many television shows made it seem so easy and quick to solve cases. Yet in reality, even with the vast resources and strength of the FBI, solving cases took time...time we did not have considering the longer these boys were not found, the less likely we would find them alive I feared.

"There is another issue we have to discuss," I said. "The three boys kidnapped have severe needs and thus are all on at least one kind of medication. If the boys don't receive their medicine, their health could be in serious jeopardy. So far, all of the parents are hugely concerned about this detail. So, I know what I'm going to suggest goes against every confidentiality and privacy law of schools and other institutions, but this is an extreme situation."

My boss, Travis Bingham, whom I had asked to attend this meeting for this reason, rose his eyebrows.

"I am going to suggest that we communicate through the media directly with the kidnappers so that they know what medications to give the kids."

Bingham, always a stickler for the rules, blurted, "No way! We could be opening ourselves up to so many legal ramifications and lawsuits. What if one of the kids dies? Think about it. How would the kidnappers get the medications? They'd have to use illegal means."

"I know this is irregular," I said. "But we've never had a case quite like this. I think we need to consider this."

"I think he's right," said Noto. "At the media, we do have ethical standards; I know, I know, that sounds weird coming from me. However, we know there is a time and a place to bend the rules. Also, if the kidnappers do try to get the medications and someone notices something suspicious, we might be able to track them that way."

That got several of us talking. We were the FBI. We probably could put several pharmacies on surveillance and catch our kidnappers that way! Man, I was less and less regretting having Noto tag along. She was becoming such an asset to this investigation. Even Bingham seemed to be warming up to this benefit of using this idea.

"I am friends with Lacy Banks from the channel 11 news," added Noto. "I'm sure she would be willing to do the broadcast."

"I concur," added Sparks. "We need to be willing to think outside the box in order to get things done with this extremely unusual case!"

Bingham, whom I think knew that Sparks had wanted his job for a while, seemed ready to retort so I interjected, "Just think about it for a night."

"Ok, I'll think about it," he said. "I don't like this idea. If, and it's a big if, we do this, we'll want to get a release signed by the parents in case something goes wrong."

We reviewed the case a while longer looking over other files, but none of our leads seemed very promising.

***

The next night, the 8 o'clock news anchor announced about the medications that the boys were on. The anchor, Lacy Banks, asked that the "kidnappers show compassion and provide the appropriate care to Adam Aaron, Kenny VanderPlaats and Ronald Meacham."

Bret Stevens watched while in his bed as he got ready to retire for the night. He figured that they might broadcast this on the news. However, he was a step ahead of them. Penders had hacked into the individual school districts' websites and ascertained the boys' medical histories and their complete Individual Education Plans. In fact, Stevens was still working on the boys with their goals. He knew all their allergies, various ailments, behavioral tendencies and how they learned best. Trying to figure out how to improve their education plans was his major goal. How he had loved being a teacher, and it was what he had always wanted to do. Education was so political, and this infuriated him! Teaching was what he had wanted to do, and he refused to let the education establishment keep him down.

***

Jen Noto felt conflicted as she drove along the highway en route to her mom's one-bedroom house. She had always cared for her mom even though the woman was a burden. However, Jen never really felt that strong of emotions for anyone else. Her professional life had always been about getting the story. She was prepared to do anything necessary to achieve that end. The people in the story or that she had to deceive to get a story never really mattered that much. When she and Graham had had the conversation after the first kidnapping, she had actually felt a small measure of guilt for the role she had played in bringing embarrassment to his wife's memory. Now she felt a real connection to the kidnapped boys. She didn't just want the story, she wanted them found! She had always believed that a conscience would be her undoing and was a crutch of the weak. Now it was really nagging at her

When she knocked on the door of her mom's one-story home, her breathing accelerated like an automobile engine of a car cruising down the highway. These visits usually did not go well.

Her mom let her in the house and smelled of strong liquor.

"It's about time you showed up to visit your old lady," Barb Noto said.

Never knowing if her mom was serious or joking, Jen played along and assumed the best.

"Mom, it is good to see you. I've missed you."

"Come on in baby," Barb said. "I want to show you my latest art work."

Her mom always had some new art work to show her. Art was one of the few things in life that gave her mom some sense of stability and happiness. Barb led her to the studio at the back of her house. The only thing was her mom's paintings were always so depressing. Her work truly reflected her emotions.

"Mom, they look great," Jen lied.

"I want to show my work to the museum. They'll accept it this time."

Jen's closed her eyes in frustration. Since she was being dishonest with her mom, her mom would once again think that the museum would accept her work. Except for a few of her best pieces, the museum turned her down, and her mom usually would go home and resort to her constant escape from her problems, her alcohol. However, if Jen was honest with her mom, then her mom would continue to emotionally abuse and control her as she always had. This cycle was never ending!

"I keep telling you to pursue your dreams," said Barb.

"Yes you do, Mom. That's why I am a reporter."

"Is that what you really want? Is that your real passion?"

Just to steer the conversation away from her, Jen asked if she had talked to any of her other family members. Her mom then went into a griping monologue about how none of Jen's sisters ever called her. They had families and some of them also had good jobs. However, her mom's last question had struck a nerve.

As the day went on, Barb ended up making Jen a sandwich, and the two talked for a while. Jen actually found herself enjoying this woman's company.

While driving home, Jen began thinking about her life. She was 40 and had been a journalist for nearly 18 years. Was it time to do something else?

***

Rick Penders sat with Adam while the boy diligently played Ms. Pac- Man on the computer. Penders marveled at how talented this boy was in front of anything electronic.

Stevens walked by. "Rick, make sure you watch this kid like a hawk on the computer! I don't want him trying to contact anyone."

"Relax man, you've paid the best in the business to run your security. I've hacked into top level terrorist organizations when I served in the army, man! I've designed software security for the Pentagon, White House and even the CIA–"

"Yes, yes, yes, I know your resume, Penders. That's why I hired you. Just don't underestimate this kid. He is a savant on the computer."

"Bah, he didn't hack into his and the other kids' district mainframes to find out their medication logs, education histories, IEPs. I'm the bomb man!"

"All right, all right, sorry I brought it up," stammered Stevens. "Let's not talk anymore in front of him. He is probably processing everything we are saying!"

Stevens wandered off, and Penders murmured, "Chill out wuss!"

***

Adam Aaron felt super anxious as a mouse about to be chased by an army of cats would feel. He missed his mom, dad and twin brother, Andrew. His twin brother always took care of him at school and made sure he was okay. He had to see his mom, dad and brother! Just had to! He flapped his hands as he thought about them. He had to control himself or he might get shocked by the stick like the two other boys had been. That looked painful! He could not get past King Koopa in the basic Mario game he was playing because he was so upset!

Just then Pender's smart phone rang. "Hey baby, what's going on?"

"Yeah, I've got a minute to talk."

Penders left the room, and Adam perked up. He closed the window of the game he was playing, and his hands flew across the keyboard. Numerous symbols and visuals dashed through his mind as he contemplated how to email his school. Something was wrong with this computer. Every time he tried something, he read "Access denied." Even though he could not read those words, he knew it meant that he had failed. He tried over and over again and had the same result.

Adam bawled uncontrollably and then punched the keyboard. Tears flooded the desk as Adam tried not to hurl the computer across the room. At his old school, when he had a tantrum, his teachers would put him in a weird room he remembered being called a cool down room. That room had squeeze machines, booster balls and other toys to help calm him down. Here at this strange school, they would hurt him! He must calm down, must calm down, he had to protect himself, the other two new friends, and get help.

***

Penders walked back into the classroom 15 minutes later, and Adam was off the computer and making statues with the Play-Doh. Penders was surprised that this little bugger was off the computer. This kid never seemed to tire of his computer time. He noticed that the kid's eyes were red; he had obviously been crying. Adam's eyes stared very hard at the computer.

"Hey, you didn't try anything when I was gone, did you?"

Adam did not respond, but Penders checked the history and smirked. "Been trying to break through my block, huh little punk?" Penders laughed harder. "Kid, I have my PhD in computer science from Yale. I've worked for the best computer companies around. You're good, but your talent is raw man. You can't beat the best."

Adam began yelling, "Want to go home, want to go home, Andrew, Andrew, Mom, Mom, Dad, Dad!"

"Not my call, son," said Penders.

***

The stress of the case was getting to me. As if that was not enough, I could not get over the increasingly growing possibility that Armon Luck really was my wife's killer after all these years. It seemed as if his nurse, Anne Potocki, may very well have covered for him. By shutting down the security cameras outside Armon Luck's bedroom and claiming she had administered his meds during the time of my wife and daughter's deaths, she had covered for him. Luck certainly had the motive for murdering Sharon; she was his doctor and he could not have her. However, why would Potocki help him? The case file had said that Luck did not come from a great deal of money. So it seemed unlikely that he could have bribed her to shut off the security cameras and lie to cover him. Darn, if only I could question Armon Luck! I may be able to tell if he was lying to me regarding the night of my wife's murder. This whole conflict of interest policy was hindering me getting to the truth! I tossed and turn until sleep finally overtook me.

Chapter 11

Annabelle Hernandez sipped her smooth Organogold latte, as she prepared to go about her daily schedule. She was anxious as reflecting on all the holiday shopping she had to do. Even though December was a couple of months away, shopping for kids these days was such a drain on families! Nonetheless, her children meant everything to her. Still, there were parties to attend, baking to get done and yet the Winter break would not begin until Dec. 22.

 Since she was the custodian for Birches Elementary School, she would not even get a full break. She sighed, as she logged into her desktop computer. As she did this, she said a small prayer for Adam Aaron, the kidnapped autistic child from this school. As a reward for good behavior, Ms. Smith would often bring him into her office for his reward time. He enjoyed playing with her equipment and especially, her computer. The small child always warmed her heart and she prayed fervently that wherever he was, he was okay.

She accessed the desktop on her computer home screen and clicked on the Internet Explorer symbol. She then browsed over her emails deleting junk mail until she got to the principal's daily to-do list. There was one email that staired back at her and was quite strange. The subject heading read "<". Why would someone email her a subject with the heading of a yellow carrot symbol? This was very strange indeed. This was probably another advertisement or perhaps one of those emails containing a virus. She was about to delete the email, but something in the depth of her soul told her not to. There was something strangely familiar about this message. She sighed and clicked open and the email read "Bd mce, "squ," and "wht sqr". Was this some kind of joke?

No, this was familiar. Where had she seen this before? She scrolled to the bottom of the email and read the word "Adam."

Adam! Yes of course! This was from Adam Aaron, her buddy! When he was playing on her computer for his reward time, he often would type random words but leave out letters of various words like he had in this email. Oh my gosh, the boy was alive, he was alive! She yelled out and jumped up like a kangaroo fleeing from a predator. She had to get the principal!

***

I sat at a local bar with Jen Noto, and we discussed a variety of topics. This woman was actually very pleasant to talk to. She was quite a sports fan and very into 1980s music and culture. Talking to her definitely took
my mind off of my personal problems and this bizarre kidnapping case. We even dove into some of our personal demons. I talked about how much I missed my wife, Sharon, and my daughter, Angela. She talked about her alcoholic mom and how her mom's circumstances possibly contributed to her clinical depression.

"I think I am destined to turn into my mom someday," said Noto.

"You are in control of your destiny," I said silently cursing myself for the cliché.

"Everybody says that!" whined Noto.

"Yes, but unlike everybody else, I actually have a clue as to what you're going through. Even though my depression is situational, I experience the same emotions. You know, usually talking about my depression doesn't help, but talking to you is actually therapeutic."

"Hmm, I guess that's why alcoholics are part of Alcoholics Anonymous," said

Noto. "Speaking to people that we can relate to really does help sometimes."

As we were talking away, my phone buzzed. I rolled my eyes, as I silently communicated to Noto what I had to do.

"Whoever invented cell phones let alone smartphones should be stoned!" stated Noto.

"For sure!" I added.

As I read my text, I nearly dropped my phone into my drink before securing the bobbling phone.

"What is it?" asked an incredulous Noto.

"Here is money to pay for lunch. It looks like we may have the first serious break in the case. Enjoy your food; I've got to go."

"Hey, whoa whoa, don't even think about shutting me out!" bellowed Noto. "Remember our agreement."

I was about to lay down the law with her, however, I realized she was right. "Yeah, yeah, ok, come with me. Just remember your end of the bargain!"

***

Noto, Ken Thompson and I were headed back to Birches Elementary School in Mapleville, Maine. Supposedly Adam Aaron had made contact with the school. The custodian, Ms. Annabelle Hernandez, had received the message. My heart pounded like an overheated furnace, as I struggled to stay within the speed limit. Three days had elapsed since the last kidnapping, and we desperately needed to make progress. However, it was also important that we keep a lid on this. My better judgment told me to insist that Noto stay away, but she had suckered me into letting her tag along. Why do we men always allow women to manipulate us so easily? I fervently hoped that I would not pay for allowing myself to trust this woman who had so angered me in the past.

The three of us quickly and discreetly entered the school and were escorted into the principal's office while our tech team immediately began analyzing the computer in the custodian's office to ascertain the origin of the email. Mrs. Carrier, a no-nonsense woman in her forties, paged Ms. Hernandez and Ms. Smith to the office. Mr. and Mrs. Aaron were already sitting in the office.

I shook their hands. "Good to see you again Mr. and Mrs. Aaron." Their mood was noticeably better but guarded because of this new development.

"This is such a relief for both of us!" said Mrs. Aaron. "We have not slept in three
days. At least we now know he is alive."

"Absolutely," said Agent Thompson. "We've been sure all along that whoever
took Adam and these other kids did not mean to physically harm them."

A minute later, Ms. Hernandez and Ms. Smith, whom I had interviewed previously, entered the office.

"Welcome everyone," began Carrier. "We have received this email that is an attempt at communication from Adam Aaron. I would like everyone to read it and share their ideas."

Thompson was the first to read it then declared, "This makes no sense! It's just a bunch of random misspelled words that are color coded!"

"That's where we think we can work together," said Carrier. "Ms. Smith and Adam's parents can shed light on what this might mean."

After I read it and then Ms. Smith read it, she said, "This does make sense! Adam has a high level of autism and these children tend to be very visual and see the world in a visual way."

"Please elaborate," I said to Ms. Smith who seemed to be looking to me for permission.

"Adam loves colors and often uses colors to describe and makes sense of his world. He color-coded the carrot symbol in the subject heading and many of the other words in the email yellow. Yellow is his way of saying something is wrong. He doesn't like yellow, so I think he is using that color to communicate that he is in distress."

"Oh no!" wailed Mrs. Aaron. "Do you think he is being hurt?" Her husband rested his hand on her shoulder to support her.

"I'm sure he's fine," I said. "Remember, I explained that I think the kidnappers are keeping him because they have some connection to kids with special needs. I don't think they are hurting the kidnapped boys. Ms. Smith, please continue."

She then explained, "The words 'wht sqr' might mean white dry erase board. He always seemed to love the dry erase board in my room. He often calls things he doesn't know the name of by shapes. Since a dry erase board is shaped like a square, he sometimes called it 'white square.' He's clearly describing his environment!"

"Oh my gosh!" wailed Mrs. Aaron. "What a brave child. You have to find him!"

"So whoever is holding him apparently has a dry white erase board?" I queried.

"How does that tell us anything?" asked Thompson. "Numerous people could be using white dry erase boards."

"Still," I reasoned. "Outside of schools, I don't know too many other professions where people use small dry erase boards. What about color-coding his name red?"

Everybody seemed confused by that, but Ms. Smith concentrated, processing something in her memory. She then quietly said, "That is how his name appears on his desk. I mean, *exactly* how it appears on his desk."

We all chewed on that comment, but I certainly felt that was a stretch.

Thompson then said, "Well, doesn't his name appear on other places besides just his desk?"

"Yes, it does. But Adam as well as several kids with autism do not generalize things outside their normal contexts. The thing is,

106

his name on his desk is in red letters. When he practices tracing his name on paper, it is always in a different color. Whenever he types his name on the computer, he just uses the standard black color."

"So, by color-coding it red in this email, he must be telling us that there are desks where he is being kept?" asked Ms. Hernandez.

"So it's as if he is being kept in some kind of school?" Noto asked. "This clue along with the dry erase board does make it seem like he is being kept in a school environment."

"What about the other things in the email: the "bd mce' and 'squ' that has green text" I asked.

"I think I have an idea about the 'squ,'" Mrs. Aaron said excitedly. "Based on what Ms. Smith said, I think the letters sq and u are short for square. Since it is color-coded green, he is describing something in the environment that is green." The rest of us waited patiently for her to process her thoughts and elaborate. "At home, whenever he walks by the window, he describes what he sees outside and then says window. If it's snowing outside, he'll say 'white window,' if it's autumn, he'll say 'brown window!'"

"So you think he must be saying that there is a window wherever he is being held and he sees green grass?" asked Mrs. Hernandez.

"Yes!" declared Alice Aaron.

"That's exactly what he must be saying," added Mrs. Carrier.

"Unfortunately, that does not narrow it down very much," said Thompson. "But at least we know he is not being kept in the dark like in a locked basement," added Noto.

"Very good," I said. "Now for the 'Bd' and 'mce' mention. Any ideas on that?"

"I am guessing that the 'bd' and 'mce' are abbreviations for blind mice as in the story, 'Three Blind Mice.' You see, Adam enjoyed the book 'Three Blind Mice,'" stated Ms. Smith.

"I read it quite a bit at home also," continued Mrs. Aaron.

"So is he saying that he is being held in a school-like environment where they are reading 'Three Blind Mice?'" Thompson asked skeptically.

"No," I said. "I'm guessing he's describing his environment he's being held in using the three blind mice as a metaphor."

We all chewed on that possibility as we sat quietly in the principal's office.

"So, he could actually be using the three blind mice metaphor to describe him and the two other boys," reflected Noto. "The other possibility using your reasoning is he is referring to the people holding them."

"No, I really think you are on track with him describing the three boys," I said. "They are all the three-blind mice being kept in some building, house or other establishment with a window."

"If the kidnappers are keeping them somewhere with a window, then they might be in the middle of nowhere," added Noto. "They would not keep three kidnapped boys in a place with a window if there was a risk of people seeing them."

"So they may be being held in a forest or home surrounded by cornfields," added Ms. Hernandez.

I stood and approached the Aarons. I grasped Alice's hands, and my eyes looked deep into her and her husband's eyes. "Your boy is very smart and very brave for what he did. We are going to get him back!"

***

After our meeting, we met with Jacob and Hamza, the two techies. Both were very professional and good at their jobs. I had worked numerous cases with them before. Jacob was a little socially awkward and had thick glasses, but knew what he was doing. Hamza had a youthful look, almost like a modern Doogie

Howser, since he looked so young. However, unlike Howser, Hamza was Arabic.

Cutting right to the chase, I asked, "Any luck on tracking the email?"

"So far, no!" said a clearly frustrated Jacob. Hamza then went into a technical explanation of how the boy bypassed the proxy server and then how the kidnappers then spoofed the IP address.

"So we have no idea where they could be!" said Jacob. "The boy was a genius in getting past the proxy, but the kidnappers were smart in making their account untraceable!"

"We might be okay," I said. "We've got some good clues from the email."

A few minutes later, we departed the school and I briefed Travis Bingham on our way back to the jet.

Chapter 12

Jen Noto headed to her office at the news station and felt more conflicted than ever. Suzan Ito had called her and wanted her to cover the village hall meeting. However, all she could think about was the kidnapping case and Adam Aaron emailing his school. Truth was, she had been neglecting several of her other assignments on her beat.

Before entering the building, Ito called her name and asked Jen to step into her office.

"How's your story on the kidnappings coming along?" asked Ito.

"It's coming along pretty well," Noto said. "One of the boys just communicated with the school. They can't trace the email, but he left some clues as to their whereabouts. So they should be able to find the boys soon."

"If the boys are found too quick, then the story won't be so hot."

Jen cringed at her boss' reasoning.

"That is major news right there," said Ito. "Can't you just picture the headline? *Autistic boy breaks proxy server, communicates with authorities.* This will get you the Pulitzer you've always wanted."

"But Suzan, with all due respect, running a story like this might compromises the boys' safety. Plus, I promised Mr. Graham I would not run a story on the case without his permission."

"Nonsense!" said Ito. "This story will make your career. I want a draft of your story in my email inbox by 11 tonight!"

Jen pursed her lips and poised herself for saying what she had to say next. "I'm not doing it. I made a promise to Graham, and

I intend to keep it. Plus, I do not want anything to happen to those boys because of my actions."

"If you don't run this story, then someone else will. You are my top reporter. Act like it!"

"In this situation, it is more important to be a good human than a good reporter. I am sitting on this story."

"Not a choice. It's the story or you job!"

Jen's stomach felt a rush of stress. She had known that it may come to this, but having your job threatened like that is always nerve racking. Jen took a deep breath and shrugged. "Ok, then it's been nice working here, but I guess it is time to move on."

***

Andrew Aaron lay in bed that night and once again was unable to sleep. He missed his twin brother, Adam, so much! He and his brother were so close, even though Adam could be a pain at times. Things were definitely hard when Adam would have one of his meltdowns. It was often tricky for him and his parents to settle his twin brother down. Andrew then began to reflect on how much fun it had been this past summer when he had taught Adam how to inline skate in the basement. Many people had thought that Adam would not be able to do something like that because of the balance issue. However, with time and patience, Andrew had taught his brother to do that skill. While lost in his thoughts, Andrew began crying. Why would somebody want to kidnap his brother?

His parents had wanted him to stay in school for the first few days since his brother was taken. They had said it was good to keep things normal for him. However, he just wasn't able to concentrate at school! Whenever he saw Adam's teacher, Ms. Smith, she averted eye contact with him. It was as if seeing him was too much of a painful reminder of Adam being gone. Then there was Jimmy

Phelps, who had been a jerk since second grade. He had made a comment to Andrew that "You look so sad. At least you don't have to worry about spaz boy messing up your hair." Adam walking up to Andrew and rubbing his hand in his hair was a way of showing his excitement at seeing his twin. Phelp's comment sent Andrew over the top. He had lunged at Phelps and pounded him. The school had a zero tolerance policy against fighting. Therefore, the principal, whom Andrew could tell felt terribly guilty, had had no choice but to suspend him. Andrew and his parents did not protest since being at school was just too painful for him. However, staying at home was not much better.

Andrew and his parents kept waiting for the police to call to give some indication as to the boys being found. Hearing that Adam was alive was a huge relief to Andrew, but he just wanted his brother back! Andrew had been praying like crazy to God to return his brother. He had begged and even bargained with God to send him back. Andrew could just not figure out how God could allow this to happen. His parents and Sunday School teachers had always explained that God sometimes allowed bad things to happen because he wanted people to choose to do the right thing. However, all that advice right now seemed completely bogus. Andrew, feeling completely helpless, now tried a different approach. He tried speaking directly to Adam.

"Adam, we will find you. When I find you, I will always take care of you. I love you and miss you so much!"

***

Kenny vigorously played with the lock on his bedroom door waiting for it to open. Although he had many learning challenges, he had his strengths. He was naturally able to build things with his hands even though he did not really know how he was doing it. All he did know was that he wanted to go home. He wanted so badly to go back to his old school and see his friends. He wondered how his family and friends were doing. He thought about his "girlfriend," Susie. He wanted to show off for her when he played tag. So, it was time to get out of here!

Kenny had grabbed a paper clip when Mr. Stevens, Mr. Penders and Ms. Jones were not looking. After he got his room unlocked, he would find his new friends, Adam and Ronald. Finally, the lock came loose! Kenny wanted to yell out for joy but forced himself to keep quiet. He then turned the door knob and walked outside toward Adam's room. He walked quietly as he heard Stevens and Penders laughing above him. They were apparently watching a movie. He walked quietly when suddenly, the floor squeaked. Kenny froze! However, apparently no one heard him. Phew! Kenny finished walking toward Adam's room and began working on his door. After getting it open, he walked in where Adam was sleeping deeply.

"Adam, time to wake up. Must go. Please wake up!"

Adam quickly sat up in his bed and yelled "Ahhhh, ahhh, ahhh."

"Shhhh, must be quiet. Let's go."

Adam did not seem to understand so Kenny tried to remember how his teacher had talked to his classmates who had autism. Something triggered Kenny to say "time to go home, see Momma and Dada."

"Home, Momma, Dada," responded Adam.

"Be quiet. Follow me."

"Follow me," said Adam.

Kenny was about to argue but remembered that his classmates like Adam tended to repeat what they heard other people say. Just then, Kenny smelled something very strong.

"Oooh, gross Adam, that was a bad fart."

"Bad fart," echoed Adam.

After Adam got out of bed in his pajamas, Kenny found a jacket for Adam to wear and they ventured out into the hallway.

Now Kenny was worried because he would have to get the tall kid, Ronald, to follow him.

***

Ronald felt angry as he stirred in his bed. He wanted his mom, dad and sister. No one had changed his diaper in a while. Mr. Stevens would sometimes check on him in the middle of the night and change him, but had not come by yet. At home, his mom, dad or sister would change him. He missed them! The lock on his door began making the strange noise. Was Mr. Stevens here to change him? He walked back and forth in his room and began rocking

back and forth in order to keep calm. The door then opened, and the two boys walked in.

Kenny pulled Adam in holding his wrist. Adam made his strange humming noise, and Kenny walked right up to Ronald. "Ronald, it's time to go. Time to see Momma and Dada."

Ronald did not seem to understand but instead made a grunting sound.

"What?" said Kenny who then waived his hand in front of his face.

"Oh man, Adam, did you fart again?"

Adam did not answer but ran toward Ronald's play area and began squeezing one of the toys. Kenny felt frustration but remembered his classroom at home that kids with autism seemed to love holding and squeezing things.

Kenny then took Ronald by the hand, but the taller boy violently pulled away. The horrible smell lasted, and Kenny finally

114

realized this was worse than a fart. Ronald had pooped in his pants. He remembered hearing his teachers at this bad school talking about changing Ronald's diapers. So, this older kid apparently still wore diapers. Kenny frantically searched the room and found big diapers. Now he needed to change Ronald before they left. When he told Ronald to pull down his pants, he did not respond. When Kenny trying to pull the taller boy's pants down, Ronald slapped Kenny in the face.

Kenny at first felt like fighting back but acting on adrenaline and fear, instead assumed an extreme leadership role. "Ronald, I have to change your diapers. First, I pull pants down!"

The smaller child then pulled Ronald's pants down and fortunately, Ronald did not hit him again. He remembered how his mom had changed his baby sister and undid Ronald's underwear the same way. He quickly threw away the dirty diapers and found some wipes to clean Ronald's back side. Ronald stood sucking his thumb not seeming to mind about this smaller boy changing and cleaning him.

Kenny then grabbed a clean diaper and said to Ronald, "Lift leg." Ronald now listened, and Kenny was able to get the clean diaper on. He then grabbed Ronald's pants and surprisingly, Ronald now complied and actually helped Kenny help him put his pants on.

Kenny then said to both Adam and Ronald, "Ok, now let's get out of here!"

Section 2

Chapter 13

Ａfter Noto announced to me that she had resigned from her job, I knew she was legitimate in helping us solve the case. She joined Thompson, Sparks, Bingham and me for a debriefing meeting at the headquarters building on Adam Aaron's clue. We grabbed McDonalds dinner and I ordered a Pepsi knowing I would probably need the caffeine to burn the midnight oil once again.

Our team began pouring over the various possible teacher suspects since it seemed as if it may be a teacher holding the boys. The first case we reviewed was of a John Carson in Plano, Texas. He had served 15 years on a charge of taking off his belt and beating a student. However, we could not find a plausible motive for this suspect. Our next suspect seemed to be a more likely culprit. A female teacher from Illinois had just been paroled for a prison term for having had an inappropriate relationship with middle school boys. If she were the kidnapper, than Ronald, Adam and Kenny were definitely in serious trouble.

"I don't think she's the one," said Noto.

"What makes you say that?" asked Bingham.

"Well, Adam Aaron's clue leads me to believe that this kidnapper is keeping them in a school-like setting. It's as if this person truly wants to be their teacher."

"Ok?"

"Well, if the kidnapper only wants to have an inappropriate relationship with them, then why set up and re-enact a classroom setting."

While several agents seemed skeptical, this "outsider" – this journalist – had an amazing insight. She was truly contributing to this investigation.

"I think I know what we need to do," I announced.

Bingham, Noto and everyone looked at me with expectant eyes.

"I think we need to go public with this newest clue."

Everyone gasped, including Noto and Bingham.

"Are you sure that's a good idea?" said Noto. "Won't that tip off the kidnappers that we are on to them?"

My respect for this woman was definitely growing. "Well, I'm thinking that if there truly is some teacher gone mad, someone will have seen something or know something. Some former colleague will remember something. Also, if someone remembers seeing someone buying teaching supplies that seemed suspicious, it may give us a clue. I know this is risky, but this may be a situation where the benefit outweighs the risk."

Travis Bingham said, "Ok, that's fine if we go public."

"Let's talk about the other plan of action I think we need to take," I continued. "Since it seems that the boys are being kept in a school-like setting, I have tasked the analysts to search records of abandoned schools or other kinds of buildings."

"That sounds good," said Ken Thompson. "Are we looking at mainly schools or factories?"

"Factories?" said Jonathon Sparks.

"Yes," I continued. "Because I am thinking there may be a good chance that they are being kept in an abandoned factory. I've heard about factories in this region where they have living quarters and even classrooms for the workers' kids. Since the recession and outsourcing of manufacturing jobs, several of these factories have been simply abandoned."

"Excellent!" said Bingham. "Let's get to work and have another debriefing in 24 hours."

***

Alice Aaron walked through a cloudy dimension and felt conflicting emotions. The stress of the last few days was wearing on her but she felt a strange sensation of hope. She continued walking through
the cloudy expanse and saw a light up ahead. It was Adam!

"Adam!" she screamed. Alice began running, but her legs would not move as quickly as she wanted. She reached fervently for him, and he seemed to be reaching back for her. She was getting close to him but then sensed him pulling away from her. He then evaporated into a gaseous form. "No!" she screamed.

She then woke up in a cold sweat next to her husband and best friend of 12 years.

"Oh, Adam!" she wailed.

Ben then sat up and rested his hand on her shoulder. "Another nightmare, huh?"

"They won't go away! I just want our baby back!"

Just then, Andrew ran into the room for he too was crying. "I hate God!" he yelled. "Why would he let this happen?"

Alice embraced her son fiercely. "Bud, it is ok to be mad at God. But we must still have faith in him and not stop loving him. I admit, I have been mad at God too these past few days and have come close to losing faith. However, God tells us to trust in him even when times are bad."

"Remember in Sunday School when we talked about David from the book of Psalms?" asked Ben.

"Yeah," said an unenthused Andrew.

"David complained and cried out to God, but still had faith in him. We have to try that too even though it is extremely hard right now."

"So I can yell at God?" asked Andrew.

"Absolutely," said Ben.

Alice again directed her thoughts back to her missing son and reflected on his early years. Some people had speculated that it might have been because of Adam not getting enough oxygen when she was pregnant with her twins that had led him to being developmentally delayed and ultimately, having autism. However, many doctors were skeptical of that theory. They really did not know what had caused Adam's autism. She remembered how she and Ben had initially thought that the toddler, Adam, was simply being a good boy by watching TV all by himself while Andrew was much more energetic. However, things started to seem odd when Adam would take the toys he was given and go play by himself. He also never made eye contact as a two or three year old and they thought this seemed strange. So, Alice had begun to research about the possibility of Adam having autism and then got him officially diagnosed so they could get insurance help. She had initially thought that Adam could overcome much of his limitations, but had learned over time that she had to be more realistic about certain things. She then thought back to the dream she had just had. She sensed that if dreams truly did have an intuitive quality, that she was close to finding Adam. This dream made it seem as if Adam was making a move to get close to her but just needed a little help.

***

Kenny led the boys down to a large basement. It smelled badly like his basement at home. There were cobwebs everywhere, and it was dark. Kenny had always been afraid of the dark. Even at home, at least when he was with his mom, she let him have a night light in his room. His dad always told him he had to learn to be a big boy and not use a night light. Right now, he had to be brave like he needed to be at his dad's house. He had to think like a big boy. The boy with Downs syndrome squinted, frowned with a determined look and moved at a rapid pace between tractors, farm equipment and big boxes of items. He held on tightly to Adam's and Ronald's wrists as they moved stealthily through the maze-like storage area.

Just then, Kenny heard something strange. It was a weird squeaking noise. The boys stopped suddenly and Kenny looked at both of them. "Shhhh!"

They waited, and everything seemed strangely quiet. Just then, a small dark shadow scampered in front of them. Then another. And another!

After Kenny's eyes got adjusted to the dark, he could see more clearly. They were rats! He screamed uncontrollably, let go of the two boys ,and buried his hands in his face. The last thing he saw before covering his face was a whole army of rats coming at them!

Just then, Kenny felt himself being lifted off the ground. He opened his eyes and noticed that Ronald was carrying him and Adam in the opposite direction! Ronald ran super-fast like a rabbit being chased by a fox with the two smaller boys tucked under his arms. The army of rats were gaining on them! Kenny remembered his parents telling him that rats were poisonous. Would they bite the boys and hurt them badly? Just then, Ronald found a room with a broken lock and ran into it very quickly. One rat made it in just before Ronald dropped the boys and slammed the door shut. Kenny froze hoping that the one rat would run away. However, it then ran toward them! "Ahhh!" screamed Kenny. The rat charged Ronald and ran up his pant leg! Kenny continued to scream and feared what this monster would do to them. Just then, Ronald grabbed the rat by the tail and hurled it through a glass window super-fast! Ronald wandered around just a bit to get himself calm. After about a minute, he sat down and found a wood chip to chew on.

"Ronald, that is so gross!" yelled Kenny, who still felt upset after being chased by the brigade of rats. Adam ran in circles in this empty room and echoed "gross." Ronald continued chewing on the wood chip and eventually chucked it in the air. Kenny took several deep breaths and reminded himself that he needed to be brave now. The real- life boogey men and woman were still in this building. He had to be brave and get his friends, Ronald and Adam, out. The door that contained the window where Ronald had thrown out the rat had writing above it. It said Dock 2. Kenny had no idea what that meant but had to figure out a way to get this super large door open. There was no handle on it, just a chain with a lock on it. He then grabbed a small ladder and climbed up it to look out the now broken window. He studied the window and noticed that there was a parking lot and forest out there. They just had to get out there somehow! Maybe they could all climb the ladder and jump out. Probably not. Even if he could get Ronald and Adam to climb the ladder and them jump out the window, they would be badly hurt from the fall. *Darn!* Kenny began crying for he had no idea how they would get out of this building. Mr. Stevens, Mr. Penders, and that mean Ms. Jones would find them anytime now and punish them. She would probably use that electric thing and hurt them badly. His crying got harder and then Adam walked up to him and said, "Hi." Why was

Adam saying this? Kenny wondered if that was Adam's way of trying to make him feel better.

"We have to get out of here!" said Kenny. "We are trapped, and I want to go home!"

"Mom, Dad, Andrew," said Adam who then scampered off and went to a desk and began playing with and spinning writing instruments on a desk. Ronald continued chewing and throwing various objects, as he too was clearly angry.

"I need you guys to help me!" said Kenny angrily.

Adam, who was now lining up objects on this desk, pulled out a key and placed it alongside the other objects. Kenny looked at it and wondered what it belonged to. He stroked his chin as he pondered what this key might belong to. Suddenly, he had an idea and hope! He looked around for a lock on one of the doors. Unfortunately, the key had no effect on any of them. Kenny began panicking again, and then his spirits soared as he saw a forklift sitting close to the door. Of course! His dad had a few times taken him to work when Kenny had stayed with him. Mr. VanderPlaats had then allowed him to ride along, as the father had operated the gigantic machine. Kenny remembered his dad unplugging the forklift before using it and then plugging it in again after finishing with it. He had watched carefully as his dad drove it, operated what he had called the prongs with a lever, and everything else his dad had done. Kenny ran to the forklift, opened the door that was surprisingly unlocked and went behind the wheel. The key fit! Now he just had to plug it in to make it work. His dad had said that it usually takes about two hours to charge a forklift. So he found the plug and was surprised at how heavy it was! He was about to give up but thought about his baby sister, him mom and dad, and the bad people keeping them here. He then let out a yell and used all his might to shove the prongs of the charging plug into the wall outlet. Next, he had to find something long enough to reach the gas pedal in the forklift for Kenny's legs would not reach it. Kenny looked around for several minutes and finally found a pile of wood. There was one piece that would be long enough to reach the pedal, so this determined kid placed it on the driver's seat.

Kenny knew he had to think things through. He looked at a clock on the wall, and it read 2 a.m. He worked hard to apply the math he had learned in school and added two hours. Since $2 + 2$ equals four, then that must mean that after charging for two hours, the forklift would be ready to ride at 4 a.m.! Invigorated by this hope, Kenny ran to Adam and Ronald and explained to them what the plan was. Ronald did not seem to understand, and Adam mainly repeated what Kenny said. Kenny then touched Ron and said, "You're it." Ronald seemed to understand and began chasing Kenny. This should keep him happy until 4 a.m.

Chapter 14

Joe Reigler paced in his bedroom back and forth wearing his bathrobe. He gulped down a glass of warm milk hoping it might help him sleep. However, there was no way he would be able to lie down and get to sleep with what was now on his mind. The news report he had witnessed only hours earlier had stirred him to the core! The guilt he had lived with the past several years overwhelmed him and he felt it would crush his soul like an avalanche of snow from a tall mountain in Alaska! The news bulletin about the missing special needs students made him wonder. Could his former friend and colleague really be behind such a bizarre and awful kidnapping? He tried to reason his way out of calling the FBI tip number, but that would not be good. Could he go for another 10 years of feeling guilt? No, that would probably send him to an early grave. He took several more deep breaths and picked up the phone.

***

I guzzled down my second cup of coffee, and was awaken from my sleep by Bingham. Some man in Grover, Illinois, supposedly had a tip regarding the missing boys case. So far there had been three other leads since the
newscast about the kidnapper possibly being a teacher. Hopefully this wasn't just another wild goose chase!

I arrived at the headquarters building, and Bingham and I put on our head phones, as we were put through to Mr. Joseph Reigler. "This is Agent Mark Graham of the FBI."

Reigler cleared his throat. "I was a middle school teacher 10 years ago at Grover Ups Middle School with a man named Bret Stevens. He taught in the multi-needs classroom and was one of the most dedicated and passionate special educators I'd ever met."
I rolled my eyes hoping this monologue would not drag on too long.

"Anyway, he had an excellent career until something awful happened."

"Please continue," I said trying to mask my impatience and hoping he would get to the point.

"He was accused one day of having an inappropriate relationship with a female student. He shortly after that got fired."

This development slightly raised my attention, but I still needed much more information before considering this a plausible lead.

"I personally don't feel that he did it. Stevens was one of the most professional and dedicated teachers you'd ever meet."

"Well," I said, "sometimes when we think we know someone, we really don't. Do you have any evidence or reasons to believe he was innocent of this crime?"

"Well, here is the deal. He had a girlfriend at the time named Suzanne Gochie."

When he said this name, I immediately recognized the last name. She was the daughter of one of the richest men in the U.S. Wall Street tycoon Thomas Gochie, a famous self-made billionaire, ran one of the most successful businesses in the world. He had been fairly poor as a child but had pulled himself up by the bootstraps and became supremely wealthy.

"Well, she and her dad were obviously very well connected in the town," Reigler explained. He paused before continuing. "I know Bret and Suzanne had a fight and broke up. I honestly don't know the details, but the spurned Suzanne Gochie used her influence to get the principal to get him fired. The principal gave him bad and bogus evaluations and used that as justification to terminate his employment."

"Do you have any idea what they fought about that lead to the breakup?"

"Again, I have no idea. Whenever I asked Bret that same question, he always clammed up."

"Ok, so go on with your story. What happened next that leads you to believe that Stevens fits the profile of our kidnapper?"

"So anyway, when Stevens lost his job, he had a bit of a breakdown. He stopped eating right, sent angry letters to the administration. He even stood outside his former classroom one time and screamed, 'Those are my kids.' Well, he finally got arrested and began receiving treatment for being mentally ill."

Finally, this lead sounded like it might be legit. This Bret Stevens sounded as if he might fit our kidnapper profile, except for the military training. I also was not sure yet about how Stevens had become so well financed to conduct such an operation. Had he somehow extorted Thomas Gochie to give him money? That was possible but that that would be massive money and even a wealthy man like Gochie would not be that easily intimidated into paying that much hush or blackmail money.

"Did Stevens have any military training?" I asked.

"No, I don't think so."

"Ok, my next question involves his financial status. The kidnapper seems to have been ultra wealthy, since he surely has hired help. Was Bret Steven's wealthy?"

"Hmm. That's the thing Agent Graham. He and his family were not super wealthy when he was teaching. However, shortly after his receiving treatment for his mental illness, his life-style upgraded completely. He bought a Mercedes and some of the best clothes money could buy. Whenever I would ask him about it, he was dismissive. It was real weird man! However, he kept talking about how he missed his kids and felt that the school system and life cheated and owed him. One day, Stevens packed up and just left. He didn't tell anyone where he was going. I tried calling him but his cell phone service was cancelled."

126

"Ok, this sounds like a legitimate lead. I will contact the field agent in your area and have him meet with you. He may have some additional questions. I'll probably fly out there and definitely want to talk to the principal as well as Suzanne and Thomas Gochie."

"Please don't tell them that it was I who told you!" stammered Reigler. "They might get me fired from my teaching position and ruin my life the way they did with Bret Stevens."

"Don't worry. I always keep my sources confidential."

"I'm sure she'll know it's me. He and I were best friends!"

"We'll do what we can to protect you Mr. Reigler. However, I need to follow up on this. Three kids with severe needs are missing. They have medications they are supposed to be taking and even if they are not in mortal danger, their health and well- being are certainly at risk."

* * *

At 4 a.m., Kenny played catch with Adam with a small Nerf football that had been left in the same desk. Ronald had grown bored of the tag game and then began sleeping on the hard floor. When 4 a.m. came around, Kenny explained to Adam, "Ok, I have to go drive the forklift. Wait here, I will be right back."

"Right back," echoed Adam. Then he said "ok."

"Good job buddy," said Kenny, who then ran to the forklift and sat behind the wheel. *Ok, it is time to be brave.*

Kenny turned the key and the forklift engine began making its noise.

"It's working!" yelled Kenny.

Kenny then took the long piece of wood and pushed it hard on the accelerator and the forklift slowly began making its way forward.

Oh my gosh, how do I drive this thing?

Kenny turned the steering wheel with his left hand and the machine turned hard left. Then he worked hard to straighten it up and aim for the door that said Dock 2. He then played with the lever and the two fork prongs began going up and down.

"Oh, my gosh!" screamed Kenny.

His life truly flashed before his eyes as he gained momentum going toward the door. In one final motion, he pulled the lever so the prongs would hit the door in the mid-section. Kenny closed his eyes and the prongs contacted with the door breaking through it and making a gut wrenching sound!

"Ahhhhh," screamed Kenny for he hated loud noises.

He opened his eyes as he was now outside the building carrying the dangling door and heading toward a big medal box. Kenny quickly found the breaks and the forklift stopped and the door flew off the prongs hitting the big medal box.

"Wow!" marveled a stunned but still scared Kenny.

Ok, I must go back in and get my friends!

Kenny quickly ran back into the building through the broken opening and first ran to the sleeping Ronald.

"Wake up Ronald! We have to go!"

Ronald resisted waking up and even slapped at Kenny.

Adam then ran up and began pulling on Ronald. Adam apparently knew what was going on.

Ronald then woke up and the two small boys grabbed each of his hands and then pulled him up and escorted him out of the building.

Kenny thought about driving away in the forklift but realized that would not work. The driveway leading out of this parking lot into the forest was badly broken. Several other objects now blocked the roadway that probably led into a town! So Kenny pulled Ronald and guided him and Adam through this big parking lot with all of these strange medal boxes and then into the forest. It was still dark, which Kenny hated. However, he had to be brave and get them all to safety!

***

J en Noto, Travis Bingham, the rest of the C.A.R.D. team and I met around a conference table to discuss the latest lead about Bret Stevens, the disgruntled teacher who may well be the notorious kidnapper holding Ronald, Kenny and Adam. The field agent down in Illinois and local law enforcement were already attempting to reach the Gochies. This was the most viable lead we had come upon thus far and felt that we needed to act promptly. It was about 5:30 a.m. and my gut was telling me that these boys were in danger and desperately needed our help. I hadn't had any sleep since I had received the call from this Joe Reigler and was operating on caffeine and pure adrenaline.

"OK," said Bingham. "Where are we and what is our course of action?"

"Bret Stevens certainly fits the profile of our kidnapper," I said. "He is a disgruntled former teacher, had a breakdown after losing his job and came upon a bunch of money. The only thing that doesn't fit about the profile is he does not have a military background."

"If we can believe everything this Joe Reigler is telling us," said Sparks. "He could have his own agenda. We should look into his background."

"Well, Stevens may have paid military personnel to do his dirty work and help him snatch the boys," I said. "I'd really like to find out how Bret Stevens came onto all that money."

"Yeah, there are ways to come across money," said Noto. "There is the lottery or he may have sued the school district for wrongful termination of employment. However, there must have been some connection to Suzanne and Thomas Gochie since Gochie is a billionaire."

"Yeah, that is what I am thinking," I said. "I bet Stevens must have had some evidence against Gochie or his daughter. I think that was the real reason she manipulated the school principal to fire Stevens; it wasn't just revenge for Stevens breaking up with her or whatever. He must have been quite a threat to the Gochie family. We need to figure out what they had fought about that led to the breakup."

"Somehow we also have to figure out what evidence Stevens has against Gochie and where he is keeping it," said an analyst.

"I would actually like to go to Grover Ups to interview the Gochies," Noto said. "I might be able to notice something."

Not for this. Sparks and I will go to Illinois to interview the suspects."

Noto tensed up and her eyes glared like one would look at someone who had betrayed one's friendship.

I could tell the Noto was quite upset about being turned down from going to Illinois. So I did my best to appease her.

"I need you to stay here in case some new evidence comes to light here in Pennsylvania. Sparks and I will take the jet and fly to O'Hare airport. It is almost 6 a.m. Eastern standard time and thus, 5 a.m. in Chicago. If we leave in half an hour, we can arrive in Chicago between 7 and 7:30. I will interview the principal that fired Stevens and Sparks will try to contact Mr. Gochie. Hopefully I can catch this principal early in his school day."

After reviewing a few more of the C.A.R.D. team assignments, I reviewed what our analysts had found.

"Our analysts are checking public records of factories that have shut down the last 10 years that have living quarters and school facilities. We are figuring the boys are being kept on the Northeast Coast because of two of them being from Maine, but who knows. So far, there are eight factories in this region that match the description of where the boys might be being kept. One of these abandoned factories is in Northern Maine in a town called Cedar ville." I then went onto list the other seven, two of which were also in Maine.

"Unfortunately, I can't send very many agents to all of these factories until we have a more clear-cut lead," said Bingham.

As we exited the meeting, Noto grabbed my arm. "Mark, what is this about? You will probably need me to accompany you to Illinois to interview the Gochies and this principal! You know I notice and hear things!"

"I am sure you are quite capable, but you have to trust me on this. I need you to stay here. Jonathon Sparks and I are going to Illinois and that is final!"

"You still don't trust me, do you?" said Noto whose blood seemed to be boiling.

"Jen, don't go there. You know I do trust you. You have been an asset to the case, but Sparks is the right man for this job."

"He seems like a wise, elderly man," said Noto. "But what if a dangerous situation breaks out. Is he up to the challenge?"

"He may seem like an old man, but I've worked with him for a while. He has been in the agency for a long time and is as ambitious and tenacious an agent as they come."

"He seems kind of whiny to me," said Noto. "He kind of has an attitude that life has cheated him."

"He has been eying a promotion for several years, but he eats, sleeps and breathes this job. It is his everything. He is the man I need on my side."

Still seeming a bit hurt, she said, "Mark, there is something you are not telling me. It is my woman's intuition that you are leaving some information out."

This woman was amazing. I had studied human psychology and had been trained in what to look for in order to tell if a person was lying. This woman had no training, but just had a sixth sense about her.

I looked at her and said "I've got to get to Illinois."

***

B̲ret Stevens woke up feeling awesome. He had the sense that these boys were warming up to their new environment. Even Kenny VanderPlaats seemed to be showing signs of acceptance of him. Being a teacher was what he had always wanted to do and just completely consumed him. Stevens walked along the corridor leading to the boys' rooms like a Spring chicken on its way to breakfast. He took his key and turned the lock of Ronald's room. He entered, and everything was just off. The room had the odor of Ronald's dirty diapers, but that was quite normal. However, something else was also not right. Bret's heart skipped a beat, as he then noticed that Ronald was not in his bed! Hmmm. He calmed himself down and figured that Ronald must have only gone into the bathroom. Darn it, Bret had not checked on him earlier! Sometimes Ronald needed someone to change his diaper in the middle of the night. However, he had not needed a changing the past several evenings. So, Bret had been lazy this past night and waited until morning. It was just his luck that the one night he didn't check was the one night that Ronald would have an accident.

"Ron, Ron, come out. It is time for breakfast."

Bret walked into the bathroom knowing that Ronald sometimes needed extra prompting or physical guidance to do what he was supposed to do.

"Ronald, Ronald, are you okay?"

Bret nearly had a heart attack as he entered the bathroom and did not see the boy!

"Ronald, Ronald, where are you?!"

Ronald be in the closet? There was never any telling what this boy might be doing. Hopefully there was a logical explanation for all of this.

After two more minutes of looking under the bed, in the closets, and in the few other hiding spots in this room, it was quite obvious that Ronald was indeed missing.

Bret began crying as he was now in full panic mode.

He then scampered to little Adam's room to make sure he was okay.

"Adam, Adam," called Bret, as he rushed into the room and found the boy's bed in the same condition as Ronald's.

"Noooo!" wailed Bret.

"What are you screaming about?" asked Betty Jones, as she rushed into the room with her pistol and taser ready with Rick Penders following closely behind.

"They're gone! Adam and Ronald are not in their rooms."

"What the..." began Betty, as she, Rick and Bret were already sprinting towards Kenny's room.

After discovering the same result in Kenny's room, the three prepared to search.

"Okay, they could not have gone far!" stammered Bret. "They are just kids, and they have severe needs. They are probably still in the building. Take the walkie-talkies. Please put the guns away Betty and Rick. I do not want these kids hurt."

Betty rolled her eyes and looked condescendingly at Bret. "Look, this is what I am trained to do. I trained in guerilla warfare and this is my area of expertise. You never know what we are going to find out there or who we will run into."

"Hey, we have the tasers. That is more than enough! I order you to lose the gun!"

Betty then pointed the gun at Stevens.

"Wow, calm down!" said Rick Penders.

"Hey, I ought to fire you right now!" screamed Stevens.

"Do what you feel you have to do," said Betty while rolling her eyes. "You hired me for my expertise and because of who I am. This has practically become a military situation."

"They are just kids!" stammered Stevens.

"That attitude of yours is why they've gone missing. If you keep underestimating them, they'll find help and guess what, you go to prison!"

"I don't think they will find anyone in this forest. The nearest park ranger station is eight miles in every direction," reasoned Stevens.

"We are taking the guns, right Penders?" said Jones. However, her tone indicated that she was not really asking for Pender's permission.

"Yeah, sure," responded an unfazed Penders.

"If you fire me, I turn you in. I've done everything you've paid me to do. I expect full payment or you go down with me," said Jones.

"Fine," said an exasperated Stevens. "Just don't hurt those kids. Let's split up and report what we find. I'm sure Kenny is the leader; he is the highest functioning of all of them and very strong-willed."

As the three of them entered the warehouse portion of the factory, they saw a room with numerous loading lines, bailers and old crates. There was a desk in the corner and numerous loading docks. Stevens then saw a loading dock with a missing door. Broken glass and debris were everywhere. Just then a rat scampered past his feet. Sheesh, this warehouse had rats everywhere! Stevens had used his vast wealth from the bribery money to have toys and supplies flown in and to have professionals set up and clean the living quarters in the other warehouse in the factory but had neglected this area. The three then walked out into the loading area where there were still numerous storage trailers. They then noticed the abandoned but still running forklift. The broken dock door lay next to one of the trailers. Stevens shook his head at the lunacy of these boys using the forklift to break out of this warehouse! His panic rose for he wondered what else could go wrong on this day. The situation was unraveling and these two mercenaries he had hired were no longer listening to him! He inhaled a deep breath and briefly shut his eyes. He somehow had to maintain his cool.

"Ok, please just use your tasers if you spot any of the boys. They could not have
gone far," he said trying to sound in control and brave.

"You'll be the first to know if we find any of them," said jones. However, Stevens did not trust the sincerity in the tone of her voice.

Chapter 15

Tim Green braced himself for another full day of hiking, as he packed his backpack and added snacks. This would be the last day of this mini-three-day hiking trip he and best buddy, Ahmed, were taking. Today was Monday and they would have to return to school tomorrow after this three- day weekend. They also had to get homework done tonight. The guys had taken some homework with them, but seriously, how much can you really get done when backpacking through a forest!? Tim considered himself a true outdoorsman and had always enjoyed fishing, kayaking and hiking since he was a boy. His friend, Ahmed Mehta, was not quite as into it as he was but enjoyed it enough to tag along for one weekend. Even though Tim knew most of the paths in this maze of woods, every adventure he took in these woods brought some new discovery or route that he had not noticed before.

"Dude, hurry up! I'm not getting any younger here!"

"Chill out man! I am coming but my phone is still not working," said Ahmed.

"I keep telling you not to bring that. We are in the middle of a forest and it is hard to get a signal."

"Tim man, I don't go anywhere without this baby! She is my girl."

Tim rolled his eyes. "That is probably the only kind of girl you could get." Tim silently chastised himself for making that insensitive comment, but offered no apology.

"Hey, this is the best kind of girlfriend," cooed Ahmed. "She never talks back to me and is quite obedient," he said as he continued to try to connect to Facebook and his other apps on his Android smart phone.

Tim often had trouble understanding his peers' and other people's obsessions with smartphones. They were cool, but truly distracted one from enjoying life and nature. He had a phone since it was basically a necessity in today's world, but the device could be a pain. Although he was fairly tech savvy, phones often would not work the way they are supposed to work. He always had refused to bring his phone with him on these hiking trips. Tim did not want an electronic device interfering with his relationship with nature.

"Heck, I might not even own a smartphone someday," added Tim. "If I get the money, I may go live in a third world country completely off the grid and away from society. Sheesh, with the way the government seems to be gaining more control over our lives and with all the shootings, solitude on a desert island may be the way to go."

"Ah yes, that would be better for the rest of us not to have to listen to your ramblings," said Ahmed as he climbed out of the tent and began to take it down.

As Ahmed finished up, the two 17-year-old boys began hiking due north. The two of them had been best friends since fourth grade. Since Ahmed had had some trouble fitting in because of the color of his skin, Tim had reached out to him and the two had bonded real quick. They had double-dated during freshmen and sophomore homecoming. The two had even been teammates on the Cedarville high school football team. Ahmed was a quarterback and Tim was a linebacker. Their season had just ended a week ago. So, Tim and Ahmed were enjoying some other hobbies while they rested before the start of track season.

"What is that sound?" asked Ahmed.

"It's probably just some animals," said Tim, as he too heard the scampering feet in the distance. "You've got to learn not to get so spooked by every sound you hear in the woods." However, Tim grabbed the binoculars out of his backpacked, perched behind a boulder and looked into a valley in the direction of the running feet.

"No," said Ahmed. "I hear voices too!"

"Oh great, Ahmed is hearing voices! We'll have to find you a shrink man!"

Then Tim's jaw dropped, as he saw what looked like three humans running along a path. As they got closer, it was clear that they were humans. What was more, they were kids! What the heck? One boy appeared to be about 11 and had something unusual about his face. Oh yeah, he had Down's syndrome. This boy with Down's syndrome was holding the hand of some tall kid who was holding a young looking boy with sandy, blond hair. This was just plain weird! His gut told him that those boys were in trouble.

"Ahmed, follow me."

"What is going on? What are those voices?" "Don't ask questions man. Just follow me!"

Tim took out his Swiss army knife and began cutting through the bushes and greenery between the trees as the two guys made their move to intercept the three strange boys.

***

Kenny puffed gulfs of air! He was so tired and scared.

He wanted his mom, dad and his teachers at his real school. He began crying as he thought about them and was about to panic since he had no idea

where they were. Their three teachers from this bad school were after them. "Mom, Dad, please help!" Kenny finally screamed out. He was also tired from having to always guide the other two boys, especially Ronald. Ronald a few times plopped on the ground and was hesitant to get back up. Kenny had had to pull him hard to get him to stand up. Plus, Ronald kept wanting to stop and eat the leaves.

Suddenly, two bodies jumped out from the trees and grabbed the three of them. Two big guys with back packs grabbed the three of them. The guy with the white skin grabbed Ronald and Adam and the boy with brown skin grabbed Kenny.

"Shhh, shhhh," said the white skin boy as he held Ronald and Adam. "My name is Tim. This is Ahmed. Keep quiet, someone is after you guys."

"Bad teachers," sobbed Kenny.

"Here comes one of them," whispered Tim frantically.

"Ahmed, let this boy go.

What's your name?"

"Kenny."

"You are the three kidnapped boys! Ahmed, there is a man and a woman off in the distance, and they are each holding a gun! Go out there and make up a story for them."

A frantic Ahmed read the situation. Since Tim was stronger than he was, he had to hold onto the tall boy and the small boy. They both seemed so confused and were squirming and Tim was holding the tall boy's mouth shut. The Down's syndrome boy seemed to understand and was talking to the small redheaded boy trying to keep him quiet. Ahmed felt it was time to put his acting skills to good use.

He ran out onto the path and began walking toward the approaching footsteps. The man and the woman approached him indeed both had guns!

"Oh my gosh, don't shoot me!"

"Who are you?" the woman asked.

"My name is Ahmed. I'm just a kid! I've never seen a real gun before!" Ahmed did not have to act to express his fear.

"Kid, you'd better not be pulling a fast one on us!" said the woman. "We are looking for three kids. You'd better not be hiding them."

"I don't know what you are talking about," said Ahmed.

"What are you doing out here, kid?" asked the man.

I'm hiking with my friends. We got lost and are trying to find our way back to town."

Just then Ahmed heard a high squeaky crying sound.

The woman's eyes narrowed and she glared at Ahmed. "That sounds like Adam, the redheaded autistic boy."

"No, no, that's my sister, Manisha! She is sick, very sick. We can't find her medication anywhere. She dropped it while hiking and now she is having a severe attack. I am so worried."

"Listen kid, you'd better take me to this 'sister' of yours or – well, I do have the gun," said the woman.

"Ok, come and see," said a crying Ahmed. "But I am worried. She has systemic lupus, and it is very contagious."

"Systemic what?" asked the lady in army fatigues.

"It's a sickness very common in women. It's a disease where a misdirected immune system leads to inflammation and injury."

"What are you talking about?" prompted the woman not seeming convinced. "Yeah, it is very scary!" Ahmed continued. "People who have this disease often have arthritis, ulcers of the mouth, facial rash and hair loss."

The woman and the man made grossed out faces and grimaced. She also stepped away.

"My poor sister has already lost most of her hair! Please, please help me find her medication so she doesn't go completely bald. Manisha, how are you?"

"She is not doing good!" yelled Tim. "Please get back here!"

Ahmed silently thanked God that Tim heard his yell, read the situation and played along

"I actually did read about that in an anatomy class a while back," said the man.

The woman no longer had her glaring look but looked genuinely concerned and lowered her gun. "All right, just get out of here. Hope your sister is okay. Rick, let's go this way." She then got on her walkie-talkie. "Stevens, the footsteps we heard were a bunch of different kids. We could be way off track." The man named Stevens yelled on the other end and this man named Rick and this crazy woman tried to figure out the next course of action. They turned around, walked in the other direction and Ahmed nearly fainted from his flirtation with death. He truly had never had someone pointing a gun at him. What did these three people want with those three special needs kids? This was weird. After he caught his breath, his adrenaline kicked back in and he headed back to where Tim and these three needy kids were.

Ahmed ran back to Tim, who was still holding the tall boy and the small red headed kid.

"Dude, this is not good!" said Ahmed. "There are three crazy people out there looking for these kids. They have guns!"

"Oh crap," said Tim whose face indicated a look of panic.

"Nice job responding when I asked how Manisha was doing," said Ahmed.

"Who was that anyway?" asked Tim.

"That was my fictitious sister. I gave her an ailment that I learned about in my anatomy and physiology class. It affects women more than guys and I think it spooked the lady with the gun."

Tim nodded, as he seemed to have a new level of respect for his best friend. "She was real scary man. She and the guy she was with had army fatigues on. Who are these three kids?"

"I think I heard about them on the news," said Tim. "They've been kidnapped and the police and FBI are looking for them."

"What's your name bud?" Tim asked to Kenny.

"I am Kenny VanderPlaats. I want to go home!"

"Go home, go home," echoed the redheaded boy.

"Is his name Adam?" asked Tim.

"Yes, he is Adam. Adam, stop running in circles."

"The tall kid must be Ronald," said Tim. "A lot of people are looking for you guys. Police, FBI."

"Policemen with guns?" asked Kenny. "Yeah, we just have to get you to them."

Ronald began wandering and pulling leaves off of the tree and chewing them.

"Eww!" said Kenny. "That is gross Ronald!"

"Hey guys, we have to hide you. Those people are still out there!" said Tim whose fear seemed to be returning.

"Yes, we have to get them to the fort. Thank God we discovered and created that fort two years earlier," said Ahmed.

"Yeah, it's not too far from here. We'll get you there and then we have to call for help," said Tim. "Ahmed, is your phone working?"

Ahmed pulled it out and engaged the touch screen but then frustratingly shook his head. "Still no signal man."

Tim cursed and then Adam echoed the swear word.

"Sorry Adam," said Tim. Tim remembered what his mom had taught him about kids with Autism. They tend to echo or repeat what people say. He respected his mom for how dedicated a special education teacher she was but always felt that there was no way he would ever do that when he grew up. For one thing, teachers do not make a lot of money. Secondly, he did not figure he would have the patience for that population of student.

Tim then moved to redirect Ronald from eating the leaves in the trees. "Eating leaves is yucky," he said as he pulled the leaf from Ronald's hands. Ronald then moved to strike Tim but Tim said "Quiet hands Ronald."

He and Ahmed then moved to direct the boys to follow them to the hidden shelter that they had made as a fort years earlier.

"Guys, we are going to go to a place where you will be safe," said Tim. "We have snack foods there but you have to be quiet."

They then escorted the boys cautiously toward the shelter.

Chapter 16

A few hours later, Agent Jonathon Sparks and I debarked from our FBI jet and headed for the small town of Grover Ups. Through the area field office, we obtained the information on the location of the Gochie mansion. After Googling the name of the school where Reigler and Bret Stevens had taught, I knew the address. We also found that Suzanne Gochie was out of the country; the super wealthy can pretty much travel whenever and wherever they want. We had contacted the embassy in Spain to help us locate and question Suzanne Gochie about her relationship and fight she had had with Stevens. However, it would take time for us to jump through the red tape to actually have someone find and question her. For now, I headed toward the school and Jonathon Sparks headed for the Gochie mansion.

***

Agent Jonathon Sparks approached the Gochie mansion with caution. His mansion seemed like it was right out of a medieval manor. The bushes were landscaped to look like Greek creatures and fierce animals. Must be nice to have this kind of money! In his experience, rich people were not really to be trusted. They often thought they were above the rules. Their attitude often was that everyone else owed them and were there to serve them. After going through the red tape of arguing with the security guard, Thomas Gochie finally came to the door. He resembled the founder of Microsoft, Bill Gates.

"What can I do for you?" asked Gochie.

"Just have a few routine questions to ask you," said Agent Sparks. "Does the name Bret Stevens mean anything to you?"

Sparks could tell he had struck a chord with the old man. Gochie's facial expression and body language indicated extreme discomfort.

"Ah, that name sounds vaguely familiar. Should I know him?"

"You don't know one of the guys that your daughter dated?" asked Sparks.

"My daughter has always been very independent and self-sufficient. She has a high position in my company and does many of her own things. I am a busy man and don't keep track of her personal life very well. We are both quite busy."

"So you don't know Bret Stevens?" asked Sparks.

"Again, should I?"

"Mr. Gochie, we could play games here, but three children are missing. We have reason to believe that Stevens is our prime suspect for being our kidnapper. If you have information that could assist us in finding him, you'd better tell us. Or else no amount of money will get you out of the obstruction of justice charges we'll throw at you."

Gochie gave Sparks a smile as if he were a teacher looking disappointingly at a student. "Now son, let's not jump to conclusions. Keep in mind that I do have the best lawyers in the country to draw from..."

Sparks lost it. "You arrogant prick! Three boys with special needs are missing! You wealthy people think you are above the law! Well, if the justice system won't bring you down, we'll tell the media about your alleged involvement with this kidnapping case. The media will crucify you and your image and what would that do for your corporate empire?"

"Temper, temper son!" said Gochie.

144

One of his security guards rushed into the room and looked like he might be ready to attack Sparks. "Everything ok here?" asked the guard looking like a pit bull ready to attack Sparks.

"Yeah, yeah, we're fine," said Gochie in a calm voice. Sparks could tell that he had gotten to Gochie with the threat about ruining his business. There was just something about the wealthy and always making more money.

As the guard hesitantly left, Gochie cautiously approached Sparks. "Son, so are you interested in money?"

"I am *always* interested in money. However, right now I am more interested in saving three innocent children."

Gochie seemed to be sizing Sparks up. Finally he sighed and said, "All right, I'll cooperate with you. Let's step into my study room."

Sparks felt a bit apprehensive being led deeper into the layer of a potentially dangerous man. This was not just any dangerous man, but one who could certainly make him disappear and afford to get away with it.

Gochie led him into an office that had a first-rate desk, a conference table, pristine chairs and books circling the perimeter of the study on shelves from the bottom of the study to the ceiling! This reminded Sparks of the scene in Beauty and the Beast where the Beast showed Belle the castle library.

"I can tell you what I know, but you have to promise not to go to the media."

"I can make no such promise. However, if you are straight with me, I will not go out of the way to ruin you."

Gochie sighed and seemed to be weighing his options. "Ok, I remember Bret Stevens. He was a young, idealistic teacher in our community. My daughter had dated him for about a year. She was young and immature, but an overall good kid." Gochie shook his head as he made his next comment and momentarily had a faraway look in his eyes before regaining his composure. "Yes, my daughter did sometimes say and do some stupid things. Anyway, she and Mr. Stevens had a misunderstanding and broke up."

"Do you know what it was they fought about?" asked Sparks.

"I don't pry too much into my daughter's private life. However, after Stevens lost his job, he had a break down. He blamed my daughter for ruining his life and career."

"Did you play a role in him losing his teaching position?"

"No, I do believe my daughter did that. I know she was very hurt and upset by whatever they had fought about and him dumping her."

"So, did you have any contact with Stevens again after his breakdown?"

"Yes, I actually did. He talked about suing my daughter and the school district for their alleged role in his losing his job. Such an action would be a scandal to the town, the school and my business. So, I paid Stevens some money to settle the matter and hopefully appease him."

"How much money did you give him?"

"Enough to cover the money he lost from not teaching anymore, his medical costs and make him forget about being wronged. "

"How much?" Sparks added firmly.

"Enough to make him forget about losing his teaching position," repeated Gochie calmly.

"You'd better be shooting straight with me," demanded Sparks. "We are the FBI; we can obtain your balance sheets, tax records and other information from way back."

Gochie did not seem the least bit intimidated by the prospect of having the FBI threatening him. Sparks marveled at how much the rich thought they ran and controlled everything. He decided to report on this information to Graham and then decide on the
next course of action.

***

I took a seat in Principal Kyle Lodewyk's office and asked him about Bret Stevens. Lodewyk was a tall man with brown hair, a slight bald spot in the middle and sophisticated looking glasses. He wore formal pants, a button-down white shirt and a conservative tie.

"Yes, Stevens had a huge heart and really cared for this kids. He was an asset to the staff, but he just lacked many of the traits necessary to be an outstanding teacher. He had the heart and knew his methods and theories very well, but just had difficulty applying them. His instincts of being able to make quick decisions as a special education teacher were not where they needed to be."

I made mental notes on the baseline of his physical mannerisms, his breathing rate, how he positioned his head and other notable characteristics. I had initially asked him questions about when Stevens had taught and a few other questions in which we already knew the answers. Knowing how he behaved when he was telling the truth enabled me to get the baseline on how he conducted himself when telling the truth. As soon as he would begin behaving differently, I would know he was lying.

"So tell me about the event that led to your terminating Mr. Steven's employment," I requested.

Lodewyk began explaining how a couple of his paraprofessionals noticed him manhandling a few students and that this made them uncomfortable. After the administration investigated, they felt it would be in the school's and the students' best interest if Stevens was let go.

I noticed a slight deviation in Lodewyk's behavior, but nothing major. So I figured he was probably telling a half truth.

"Do you know Suzanne Gochie?" I asked.

"Well, I don't know her personally, but I know of her," he stated nervously.

"Did you know that Stevens had been dating her?"

Getting visibly shaky, he said, "Well, uh, uh, I believe he mentioned her or maybe a st-st-staff member mentioned that they were dating, but I didn't really p-pry into my employees' personal lives. It wasn't my business."

"So she and her dad did not pull their weight or any strings do have you fire him?"

Completely perspiring, he said, "I am a professional and would not let someone bribe or intimidate me into firing an employee. That is not how I run my school!"

I thanked him for his time and decided to check in with Sparks and the rest of the C.A.R.D. team to decide if we should follow Principal Lodewyk. Sparks and I convened at the headquarters field office close to Grover Ups, Illinois, and we had a video Zoom conference with the rest of the C.A.R.D. team. Local field agents and law enforcement were keeping an eye on Principal Lodewyk and Thomas Gochie.

After Sparks rehashed his conversation with Gochie, I discussed about my interrogation of Lodewyk.

After reviewing about the first part of the conversation, I explained "in addition to him being notably more fidgety after I began mentioning about Suzanne Gochie, his other mannerisms changed. So I am certain that he was lying to me. He knows Suzanne."

"Do you think it was possible that he was having an affair with her?" suggested Noto.

"Quite possibly," I said. "I am thinking that Stevens knew something about Ms. Gochie, her father and possibly Dr. Lodewyk. That was why they fired him; he was a threat to them."

"Then that was why Mr. Gochie bribed Stevens – to keep him quiet?" asked Ken Thompson.

"That's my theory," I said. "Somehow we have to figure out what Stevens and Suzanne Gochie fought about. That should lead us to what evidence Stevens had to blackmail the Gochies. That is the key. It would take enormous evidence against the Gochies to intimidate this billionaire to pay the kind of money he did to Stevens. People this wealthy do not cough up this kind of money easily."

I cracked my knuckles as I prepared to continue with the next necessary lead we had to follow up on. I continued "We are working with pubic records to track down Steven's mom. It turns out she was in a nursing home in the town. He picked her up from it right before he disappeared. The home does not know where he took her."

Noto interjected "He probably wanted to protect her from the Gochies if Stevens was blackmailing them. They might kidnap or hurt her to stop Stevens."

Bingham added "We are pursuing every database at our disposal to track down his mom, Heidi Stevens. We'll find her soon."

Bingham then sighed heavily. "Unfortunately, this is not really getting us any closer to finding the boys! What else do we know?"

Noto, Thompson and the analyst team responded by reporting on a major break of obtaining AWOL army records. After thoroughly reviewing them, they concluded that the two main suspects were deserter soldiers Betty Jones and Rick Penders. Jones had a history of having a hot temper and insubordination. She had been court marshalled at Fort Bragg but had somehow disappeared. She was also an expert in explosives, which might explain the flash grenades that had gone off at the schools. Plus, she was obviously a female as Brittney Meacham had observed and the photos at Kenny's school had shown.

Then Julie Gomez, a young and thorough analyst that I had plenty of respect for, reporter on a more disturbing find. "After analyzing her prints from the army records, we found a match for those prints in VICAP. Her prints match the profile of a serial killer that we have been searching for a while."

My heart skipped ten beats as I considered the possible ramifications of this discovery.

"After she deserted the army, she must have gone rogue!" I exclaimed. "She must be a mercenary and has been hired by Stevens to help maintain order."

"He probably doesn't know how dangerous this woman is when he hired her!" stammered Ken Thompson.

"This makes finding these kids even more urgent," I said while shaking. "They are probably in real danger! What else do we know?"

Gomez cleared her throat and continued. "Rick Penders was a computer genius who served in the Navy. He had designed security programs for the Pentagon and C.I.A. in his career. However, he was an extremely disgruntled employee who claimed he was unappreciated and underpaid. Shortly after that, he too went missing. We have no reason to believe he is as dangerous as Jones."

He and Jones would certainly be prone to being bought by someone like Stevens who could use their services.

"Ok," I said. "So let's review the possible sequence of probably events. So Bret Stevens is happily teaching in the town of Grover Ups, Illinois. He dates Suzanne Gochie, a prominent employee and daughter of Thomas Gochie, one of the wealthiest men in America. Stevens possibly notices something incriminating on the Gochies. He then threatens to expose Gochie, so she gets Lodewyk to fire him. She may also have been a spurned lover; that may have been an additional reason she got Lodewyk to fire him. After Stevens has his breakdown, he threatens to expose whatever information he has on them. Thomas Gochie, in order to protect his daughter and/or business and own reputation, bribes Stevens to keep him quiet. I'm guessing Stevens increased the blackmail amount and that is why he fled after removing his mom from the nursing home. So, Stevens, who has his heart in teaching, hires Betty Jones and Rick Penders to assist him in this kidnapping scheme. Penders hacks into the elementary schools' databases in order to find out

150

about the medications and other vital information about the boys. Jones is probably the enforcer for maintaining discipline. They bring these boys to one of these abandoned factories and use their school and housing facilities to create this pseudo reality for Stevens."

"Ok, this is quite an elaborate theory based on what we know," remarked Noto. "I overall agree with Mark. However, I am just skeptical about Gochie paying enough money to Stevens to finance this operation. I have interviewed several rich people. They don't hand out money easily as you stated earlier," she reflected. "I mean Stevens would obviously need mega millions to conduct this operation. Finding this information is definitely the key."

After diligently pouring over more databases and digging into Steven's past and family information, we found out where his mom was living! She was being kept at a nursing home downstate in Illinois. Bingham assigned Agent Sparks to fly down there and interview Heidi Stevens in hopes of obtaining any information on what information Bret had on the Gochies. We also found out that she unfortunately had dementia. This would make it that much more difficult to get any information from her. However, if Sparks could talk to her when she was lucid, she might remember something.

"I just wish we could speed up the process of checking out the factories that match the descriptions based on Adam Aaron's clues," I said feeling frustrated.

"Yeah, unfortunately with several other high profile cases that have surfaced in the last several days," explained Bingham, "Director Scheelhaase has pulled several agents in that area and does not want to deploy any agents into the towns of Baxterville, Cedarville, or Hansborough until we have more conclusive evidence that the boys may be being kept there."

"Tsss, Scheelhaase is such a politician!" exclaimed the often disgruntled Jonathon Sparks. "When this case was hot, he was all over us for solving it. Now that the media attention has died down, he doesn't care as much!"

Even though I wearied of Spark's whining, I too had to shake my head at the absurdity of the politics of the case. We needed a break to happen quickly!

***

Gloria Glen sipped her coffee as she debated about what to do. After the morning newscast that revealed about the medication that the boy with autism was on and the description of the disgruntled teacher, she was certain he matched her strange customer. The man, whose identification claimed he was Tom North, certainly matched the description of Bret Stevens. She had always been certain that he was lying to her and there just seemed to be something off about him. She certainly did not want to make a fool of herself if she was wrong. Also, she really did not want to make trouble for Tom North if he was legitimate. Why couldn't she just learn to mind her own business? However, if she was right, she would never forgive herself for doing nothing and then learning later that Tom North, aka Bret Stevens, had hurt these boys or permanently kept them from their families.

"Honey, maybe you should just call the tip number and share what you noticed," said Frank, her husband of 35 years. "Even if you are wrong, you will be able to live with yourself better if you at least report your findings."

"You're probably right. I haven't slept all night and I have been suspicious about this Tom North for a long time."

"Then it is time you do something, Hon," said Frank. "In my line of work, we rely on citizens to report to us if they notice anything suspicious."

"I'm still nervous," said Gloria.

Frank, feeling frustrated, had an epiphany and decided on a new course of action.

"I will tell you what. There is an abandoned factory in the middle of Cedarville Woods. After the management closed down the factory, it has been unused and deserted for several years. At first we would routinely check it out. We might have kids doing inappropriate things in there or drug dealers using it as a base of operations. Heh, then after our own cuts, if became a low priority. That factory, which contained living quarters and classrooms for the employees' kids, would be an ideal place to hold three boys."

"It had classrooms too?" exclaimed Gloria. "On the news, they said this Bret Stevens might be a teacher. Now I am even more sure that Tom North is Bret Stevens!" she cried with her resolve building up.

"You call the FBI tip number," Frank said. "I will take a ride to the factory and tell you if I notice anything."

***

Tim and Ahmed escorted the three boys into the fort that they had established in the woods back in middle school. They had stockpiled a ton of food to keep here for when they came on these hiking trips.

They always kept it locked in case other curious hikers felt the need to explore the inside of this fort. They also kept extra sleeping bags and air mattresses just in case they ever needed them.

Adam Aaron became very excited at the site of the vast amount of food. "Food, food," he cooed.

"I am so hungry!" said a determined Kenny.

Even Ronald began reaching for a box of the Cheez-Its.

"Ok," said Tim. "Why don't you guys sit at this table over here and we'll get you all a snack." As Tim escorted Ronald and

Adam over to the table, Ahmed grabbed some of the paper plates and rounded up the food.

"All we have is water in coolers to drink boys," said Ahmed.

"I want juice," whined Kenny.

"Sorry guys, this isn't a Holiday Inn," responded Ahmed.

"You boys will be fine. Water is good for you," said Tim. "Dude, bring over a bunch of snacks."

"I'm a step ahead of you," said Ahmed.

"Not like on the football field. Ok, we have to be serious. Those jerks are still out there. They have guns and are dangerous. They may come looking in this fort. We have to call for help! Dude, is your phone working?"

"Still no signal. I have to get closer to town."

"Crap, we are screwed!" said a panicking Tim.

"We'll be ok. I will hike back toward town until I get a signal."

As Ahmed set out the snacks, he asked Ronald what kind of snack he wanted. Since Ronald did not respond, Ahmed gave him a combination of snacks. Just then Adam raised his hand. A bewildered Ahmed said "Yes, Adam."

Adam responded with, "Yes Adam." Ahmed looked to Tim for clarification but then Adam continued. "I want cookies ... please."

As Ahmed began handing Adam various cookies, Tim said, "I think that's how they do snack time in school. My mom talked about to communicate with students with autism when doing snack time. She taught them to raise their hands and request what food they want."

As Tim watched Ahmed put various cookies on Adam's plate, something was off. There was some memory in the back of his mind that he had heard about these boys that was coming into play right now. What was it? Oh yeah, Adam had severe peanut allergies! On the news, the anchor had informed the kidnappers that

154

Adam Aaron had severe peanut allergies. Ahmed put three peanut butter cookies on his plate.

"No!" screamed Tim, as Adam picked up a peanut butter cookie. Tim moved with super speed to the other side of the table and snatched the cookie out of Adam's hand and then grabbed the remaining two peanut butter cookies off his plate.

A startled Ahmed exclaimed, "Dude, what is going on?"

"He has peanut allergies. I learned that on the news about him the other night."

Adam turned around and slapped Tim for taking his cookies.

"Hey, no hitting!" exclaimed Tim. However, Tim then remembered what his mom always said was the appropriate thing to say to kids with autism in that circumstance. "Quiet hands, Adam."

"Quiet hands, Adam," echoed Adam.

Just then, they heard footsteps outside the door!

Chapter 17

After Agent Sparks went through more red tape at Bret Steven's mother's nursing home, he headed toward the room of Heidi Stevens. The elderly home was definitely an eye-opening experience for Sparks. He knew many of them were underfunded and the workers were often underpaid. It was a huge societal issue with so many senior citizens and Baby Boomers moving into this age range. He located her room and entered while the nurse eyed him skeptically.

Sparks flashed his badge to the nurse and introduced himself.

"Hello Mr. Sparks, I don't think this harmless woman is on America's Most Wanted list."

Sparks smiled at her good-natured attempt at humor. "I have no doubt that Mrs. Stevens is not guilty of any crimes against society, certainly nothing warranting the attention of the federal government. I just have a few questions and think she may be able to help with a case we are working on."

The nurse shrugged and raised her eyebrows, as if to say *all righty* then. "Well, good luck. She has Alzheimer's and may have trouble remembering much."

Sparks sat in front of Mrs. Stevens and said, "Hi Mrs. Stevens. My name is Agent Sparks from the FBI. I just have a few questions to ask you about your son."

The woman's eyes fluttered as she had a blank look. Finally, she said "Oh, Bret, he is a good boy."

"Yes, he is, but he may be in trouble and need our help."

"He didn't mean to spill the juice on the carpet. He just was a bit careless."

Sparks smiled as he realized this would be tricky. This woman was a bit senile and had just had a flash back of Bret's childhood.

The nurse then gave him the *told you* so look.

"Tell me about his time as a teacher."

Her expression turned somber. "He loved his students. He was good to them. Ms. Gochie ruined my poor boy's life. He would never have hurt her!"

Good, thought Sparks. She seems to remember the situation pretty well.

"I'm so sorry about what happened," said Sparks. "Life can be pretty unfair. So what happened to him after he lost his job?"

"After whom lost what job?" asked Mrs. Stevens.

Sparks momentarily hung his head as he forced himself to keep in mind that he was talking to an Alzheimer's patient.

"Your son, Bret Stevens."

"Oh, yes, I have a son named Bret Stevens. He is a teacher!"

Sparks felt like he needed an aspirin right now.

"Yes, your son, Bret Stevens, was a teacher and lost his job because Ms. Gochie got him fired. What happened to him afterwards."

"He was just doing what any boy would do at that age!"

Sparks massaged his temples as he feared she was not lucid at the moment and was simply rambling. Something told him to wait her out.

"He could not turn down that kind of money."

Sparks perked up. She was clearly talking about the bribery or hush money paid to her son by Mr. Gochie."

"Ma'am, why did Mr. Gochie pay him money?" "Why did Mr. Gochie pay who money?"

"Why did Mr. Gochie pay your son, Bret Stevens, money?"

"It was just a flash drive that Mr. Gochie, his daughter and the school principal wanted gone."

***

After receiving the tip from Gloria and Frank Glen, we had the evidence we needed to move forward and converge onto the spacious forest in Cedarville, Maine. Gloria, the pharmacist, had reported about a possible Bret Stevens sighting. She figured the customer who called himself Tom North, was actually the kidnapper. Her suspicions were further confirmed when her state trooper husband, Frank Glen, drove to the factory and found fresh dirty diapers, clothes and several other things showing evidence of people currently living there. The cavalry had now been called in! The state and local police, as well as numerous FBI and even volunteers were being mobilized and sent to search the forest for our missing children. I embarked on the jet, but Jonathon Sparks stayed behind to coordinate the ongoing investigation of the Gochies and Principal Lodewyk in Illinois. I was buoyed also by Sparks's discussion with Heidi Stevens. She had mentioned a flash drive that Mr. Gochie, Suzanne and Lodewyk wanted back from Stevens. Even though the elderly Stevens had not been able to elaborate, this new bit of information clearly changed how we looked at the case. This confirmed my suspicions that Mr. Gochie was actually paying hush money to Bret Stevens. This flash drive also should show the connection between the Gochies and Principal Lodewyk, which could show why Lodewyk would fabricate a reason to fire Stevens. However, there had to be some very, very important information on the flash drive for Gochie to pay that kind of money to keep from being found. We had to somehow find out where the flash drive was located and what Stevens had on it. I also would want to find out how Stevens came upon such a flash drive but for now, finding the boys took precedent.

My jet landed, and I joined up with Ken Thompson, Jen Noto as well as numerous field agents, Hostage Rescue Team (HRT) personnel wearing Kevlar vests and full tactical gear at this abandoned warehouse in the middle of the Cedarville forest. Our forensics analysis team and the rest of us searched the remains of this old facility. We discovered the classroom where Bret Stevens used to teach the boys. Next, we discovered the manufacturing plant that apparently had been converted into a massive play room. I truly marveled at the genius of this crazy man to create such an elaborate school for these kids complete with an entertainment and play area. There were arcade games down here, a pinball machine, a mini-basketball court and several computers.

"Do you think Stevens bought all of this?" asked Agent Thompson.

I shrugged. "It's possible that some of this stuff was already here, perhaps in the break room."

Next we toured the "housing units." Stevens had used these to be the sleeping quarters for the boys.

I was actually impressed – and relieved – that this Stevens did seem as if he truly cared for these boys. Ronald's room had a container for his dirty diapers. Adam's room had a container for all of his favorite toys. Even Kenny's room had his favorite video game system in it. All of their rooms had bottles for the various medications the boys were on. So this Stevens obviously knew the boys' likes and dislikes and medical needs. He must have found that out by having Rick Penders, the former disgruntled army techie, hack into the various boys' schools. Penders probably also reprogrammed the security system at Kenny's school. Amazing!

After searching this warehouse, it became quite obvious that they were not here anymore. I had found the bent paper clip that one of the boys, probably Kenny VanderPlaats with Down's syndrome, had used to escape their rooms.

We then searched the numerous rooms and warehouses of the factory. We noticed the warehouse where it appeared as if the boys had careened their way through a dock with a forklift and then fled on foot through the forest. We noticed footsteps leading from this loading area into the forest. It was obvious that this factory had been closed a long time ago for the road leading from it to the town of Cedarville was badly damaged. Years of neglect had left the road with potholes, cracks and several trees had fallen down blocking the path. Numerous state troopers, cops and other agents had apparently already searched the remains of the road connecting to town but with no trace of the three boys or the three likely goons hunting for them. My gut was telling me that the boys did indeed navigate their way into this dense Maine forest with a labyrinth of paths. Although there was a cavalry of people searching for them, the boys were still in grave danger. I took a deep breath. Things then became about managing chaos. I shouted orders to the various members of the C.A.R.D. team.

"Ok, 'Agent' Noto. If you are going to help us find these boys, you need to have a gun."

I handed her a Smith & Wesson and as usual, the woman seemed as if she had a tough exterior.

"You ever fire a gun before?" I asked her.

"Well, yeah, but only at my dad's combat ranch in Texas."

"Well, hopefully you won't need it. Just stay close by and hopefully we'll be okay."

I sensed that everything was coming full circle. We would probably find the boys soon. I just hoped we weren't too late to find them alive!

Chapter 18

Betty Jones was on the opposite side of the shed that she and Penders believed was being used as the fort for the boys. She was on this side in order to out flank the boys. She had her Glock ready to end this mission once and for all. Things were spiraling out of control. She knew the army and military were converging upon this forest here in Maine. She had had enough training and experience to recognize when the enemy was converging upon her. It was time to leave no survivors! She was not sure where Bret Stevens was at this moment, but she knew Rick Penders was at the front door of this fort. So there was no escape for the five boys, who were surely hiding in there. So here was her plan: she would quickly and methodically shoot all five boys, end the life of Rick Penders, then escape. Penders thought they were going to simply reacquire the boys. He had no idea of her true intentions. If she saw Stevens later while escaping, she would take care of him as well. Hopefully he had already deposited his latest payment into her off-shore account. If not, Stevens still had to be removed from the land of the living. Since they had all seen her face, they had to be eliminated. She smirked as she always got a bit of a thrill when killing people. She really did not know what the big deal was. People died in third world countries by the hundreds each day. Who cared that these boys had special needs; they were useless to society anyway. Huh, if anything, they would be a drain to future tax payers. So in a roundabout way, she was doing society a favor.

"Ready, Penders?" she called.

"Yes, let's do this!" shouted Penders from the other side of the clubhouse.

The two AWOL soldiers threw open both doors and entered. Jones entered ready to fire away but saw only an empty tree house!

"No!" she screamed.

* * *

Ahmed and Tim whisked the boys stealthily through the dense shrubbery of the forest. It had turned out that the footsteps they had thought they had heard from outside the fort a while ago was only an animal. All of them were on edge and at the cusp of losing it. "We've got to go back to the fort, those creeps are after us!" whined Ahmed.

"No, dude, we have to get them out of the forest. If we stay in one spot, we are sitting ducks man!" reasoned Tim. The five of them continued moving and Ahmed did not have the will power to continue to argue.

Suddenly, they heard the woman! "Penders, I heard something straight ahead!"

Ahmed cursed and said, "That's the woman and the man!"

"Keep moving!" hissed Tim through clenched teeth. As Tim did this, Adam Aaron yanked out of the grip of his hand and bolted. "Adam, come back!" yelled Tim, not thinking about the killers in the vicinity. A frantic Tim watched as Adam disappeared into the dense underbrush of the massive trees. He would find the boy if it was the last thing he did!

* * *

Tears poured down Adam's face! Everything was so unpredictable lately! All the green leaves, tall trees; make them stop! Being interrupted in the middle of the night had thrown enough of a wrench in his routine; just as he was getting used to his new life. Now he felt like he was dying and his head was about to explode! Just then, a hand reached down and grabbed him. It was his teacher at this new school! "Mr. Stevens," Adam tried to say but the hand covering his mouth made that impossible. He then felt some cold metal being pressed to the side of his forehead.

***

I heard what sounded like a teenage boy yelling. "Stay close," I said to Noto.

"No, we should split up," she said. "He yelled Adam's name. It sounds like a teenager. I think it is someone trying to protect the boys."

"It may be one of the kidnappers trying to confuse us!" I said, not sure what to make of the strange development. There was no time to argue. "Ok, you go that way, but keep in touch. I'm calling Thompson and the others."

***

Sweat poured down Bret Stevens as he sensed everything becoming unraveled. Multiple police and FBI agents were in this forest. His elaborate plan to make himself a teacher again had failed. His life
dream had been rudely ripped away from his grasp yet again! Well, he now had to do what he had to do to survive.

"Don't move, Adam, or I'll pull the trigger."

***

I ran in the general direction I had heard the yelling coming from. However, I had never been much of an outdoorsman. When I had been on a hiking trip in boy scouts as a child, my scout leader had told the other leaders and me that he didn't want me being in the forest by myself. Yes, I had always been a bit directionally challenged. Suddenly, I heard a man's voice ahead. My adrenaline kicked in as I sensed I may be getting close to finding one or all of the boys. I was this close and would not let them slip through my fingers like I had my family! Up ahead on a path, I saw what looked like a man. This man was holding something. I moved in for a closer look gripping my gun and walkie-talkie closely. As I inched closer, like a combat foot soldier sneaking up on an enemy army, there was no mistaking what I was seeing. This man was holding a child and pointing a gun at him. After my initial bout with fear and the PTSD(post-traumatic stress disorder) from the night I encountered my wife and daughter dead, I forced myself to focus and simply do my job. I recalled the photos I had seen of the three boys and all the suspects and everything became clear. This man was Bret Stevens and he was holding young Adam Aaron at gun point. This was where things got truly tricky. If I made one wrong move, the boy could die. Also, I knew Stevens was an amateur so that made him unpredictable. I prayed a silent prayer, which I hadn't done in years, and then braced myself to calmly resolve the situation.

"Bret Stevens, don't do this!"

"Don't come any closer. I swear I will shoot the boy!"

Stevens was drenched in sweat as he held Adam and the gun tighter. Steven's eyes darted back and forth as he was on high alert.

"No please," I reasoned and actually lowered my own gun to diffuse Stevens. "Mr. Stevens, you love that boy. You kidnapped him because you wanted to educate him and help him live a better life, right?"

"Yeah, I meant well. Society and life have screwed me over. I was and am a good teacher! I did my job well."

"Yes, you did. What Ms. Gochie did to get you fired was wrong," I said while silently cursing myself for mentioning her name. I noticed Stevens clearly stiffening up and holding the terrified boy tighter while pressing the muzzle of the gun further into his head.

"Yeah, she should be the one in prison. It's because of her that I am in this situation!"

"Yes, she is," I said. "Don't let her hurt this boy. She ruined your life, don't let her ruin Adam's life. Look at him man. The boy is crying!"

Bret then began crying himself.

"I shouldn't have taken her dad's money!" he wailed.

"No, you shouldn't, but you might still be able to make things right. Do you still have the flash drive containing the evidence you have that was a threat to the Gochies?"

Bret's eyes fluttered back and forth as he was going back to a painful memory.

"You can make things right. I think you felt guilty about taking the hush money. That's why you tried using it for something good."

"What have I done?" cried Bret.

"Let the boy go. It's time to make things right."

A despondent Stevens placed Adam down who then ran in three circles and then sat on the ground.

Stevens sat down himself and continued crying.

"Stevens, Stevens, come in," said the voice of Penders. "Come on man, answer your walkie!"

Stevens picked up the walkie-talkie, and I signaled for him to just wait. I then said, "You can trick them into coming this way.

I will radio for backup and then the two other boys will no longer be in danger."

Stevens nodded warily at me and spoke into his device, "This is Stevens."

"Hey man," said Penders. "We may have spotted the three boys. There are apparently two other teenage guys helping them. Jones and I are moving in to take a closer look. We heard some kid yell Adam's name, but we think it was a ruse."

"Don't worry about it. I have all three of the kids here and I'm holding them at gun point," Stevens lied.

"Really?" gasped Penders. "Why didn't you call in then? Plus, why did you sound sad when you first answered?"

"Listen man," said a clearly agitated Stevens. "It's been a stressful day and night! I can't answer for every little comment I've made. Just get your butts back to my location and help me take the boys back."

Ten four," said Penders. "We'll be there in five minutes."

***

Betty Jones was in full hunting mode. She was ready to shoot to kill. Penders had just informed her that Stevens had called her to inform her that he had all five of the boys. However, something did not seem right. She did not trust Stevens, who always had seemed like a softy. Although she was happy about the several million dollars he was paying her, she should not have partnered up with such a mentally unstable man. She felt nothing for the three boys that they were holding. Her time in Afghanistan and Iraq had also taught her not to feel, or care. She was simply a mercenary serial killer now. Therefore, she would eliminate the boys, the men and bury them, and then get the heck out of the forest. It was time to eliminate everyone!

166

Chapter 19

Kenny VanderPlaats clung to Ronald's hand as the two boys ran through the woods. He was worried about his friend Adam. However, they had to keep moving. Real life monsters were chasing them. The two big kids that found them in the forest were standing on both the front and back of them. Tim was leading them and Ahmed was in the back making sure they were safe. Kenny felt like they were playing tag at recess. Only now, the people chasing them were very dangerous!

"Oh my gosh!" said Ahmed as he looked back.

The four of them were frantically trying to navigate their way through the trees! The woman was gaining on them! Tim and Ahmed were becoming so tired.

"We have to split up!" said Ahmed.

"No way," said Tim. "We won't be able to find each other then. We've already lost Adam..."

Just then they heard gunshots. The woman was firing at them! Tim cussed and grabbed Ronald and dove into a group of bushes. Ahmed and Kenny ran in the other direction and then stumbled upon a bunch of twigs.

***

My heart skipped 10 beats as Stevens, and I heard the gunshots. "Big trouble!" said Adam Aaron. With Stevens carrying the boy, he and I ran in the direction of the shootings and I screamed into the walkie. "Noto, Thompson, state or local police, anybody, shots fired! We need back up immediately!"

***

Penders was running in the direction of where Stevens had given his location. Now he heard shots back from where Betty had been. What was going on? Was she firing at the authorities or at the kids? Had Stevens hoodwinked him by saying that he was holding the boys at gun point? Or was Betty fooling with him? He did not know whom he could trust! Even with being a millionaire by helping Stevens out, this mission was turning out to be more than he had bargained for. He certainly did not think that helping guard three kids with severe special needs would be so difficult. Even though he had completed boot camp, he had little experience in actual battle. He was always the computer geek and working behind the scenes. Well, now it was time to make sure that he survived. So, he stopped and waited.

***

Betty Jones saw the boy with Down's Syndrome and the young hiker she had recently met with dark skin. He had pulled a fast one on her with his ruse about having a sister with that lupus disease! However, she would not underestimate him again. Both boys looked extremely scared and had their hands up. She was not going to make the mistake that villains so often make in movies by asking her captives if they wanted to have any last words. She lined up her gun and began to pull the trigger. It was time to end this and get the heck out of here. "Ow!" she screamed. Something had grabbed the back of her leg and its nails dug deeply into her skin! She looked down and it was the tall, retarded boy, Ronald Meacham! Wow, talk about an amazing million to one coincidence. She delivered a full roundhouse kick full force in the solar plexus knocking the wind out of him. Well, his efforts would be for naught as she pointed the gun at him. However, the gods still were not with her as someone tackled her full force! It was the dark skinned teenage boy that had lied to her earlier. He drove her into the ground and knocked the gun out of her hands!

"Get the gun!" screamed Ahmed. Tim began frantically searching through the greenery looking for the gun as Ahmed fought this crazy woman. Tim had a new level of respect for his friend, who was only a quarterback for the football team. Quarterbacks rarely had to make tackles.

Ahmed punched her in the face but little did this high school punk know just how thoroughly trained she was. She had been a kung Fu and boxing champion at the military. She kicked him in the privates and then open-palmed him hard in the nose breaking it and sending him flying. She then pulled out the serrated hunting knife and would have to take out each kid in a more primitive fashion. She grabbed Ahmed, who was now bleeding profusely and crying. As she got ready to cut his throat, she heard, "Betty, that's enough! I don't want anyone else to get hurt!"

That was the voice of Bret Stevens. However, he had someone else with him. It was an FBI agent with a gun now pointed at her. Crap, this changed things considerably! She now had to use this amateur teenager as a hostage.

"Don't move any closer or I'll cut the boy's throat!" she yelled.

"Betty, let them go. You can have your money. I'll put every penny in your account."

"Oh sure, like I'm supposed to believe that!" she screamed. "If I let the boy go, that FBI agent is going to shoot."

"No, I won't," I yelled using my other hand signaling her to calm down. "Please, just take it easy. I'm going to put my gun down." My heart was beating a million miles a minute. If I put my gun down, then Betty Jones had all the cards. She would be completely in control. My panic increased for I could not decide on the best course of action!

"Plus," she yelled, "how am I supposed to know you'll keep your word Mr. Stevens about depositing the money in my offshore account?"

"Betty, I've always been a man of my word! I've followed through with my plan, but it has not worked out. It's time to move on. It's time for these kids to go home."

"Look, I'm not letting anybody go until the FBI agent puts his gun down. Mr. Agent, you have five seconds to put it down!"

My usually steady hand was vibrating like a California earthquake. I tried to analyze all the scenarios, but nothing was looking good. I could not let this good Samaritan boy who had been protecting the three kids get killed. So, I knelt down showing I was putting my gun down as Jones got close to the five count.

"No, please, I'm putting my gun down," I said, as I placed it in the dirt next to me. I then kicked the gun away.

Ms. Jones then looked at me with a smirk. "Ok, now I am taking this kid and if you try to follow me, well, use your imagination."

"NO!" screamed Ahmed.

Just then, Tim found the gun and pointed it at Ms. Jones. "Let him go!"

Much to Tim's dismay, this crazy woman only smiled.

"Listen kid, if you shoot at me, I'll still have time to kill your friend."

Tim began crying. "Come on, just let him go!"

Just then Penders showed up and had his gun trained on Tim. "Well, it's about time you showed up!" barked Jones. "Now get the gun from that kid and let's get moving. We have to eliminate everyone!"

After Penders disarmed Tim, a gunshot erupted from out of nowhere nailing Jones in the shoulder. Jen Noto had lined up the shot from a distance in the tree. Next everything happened very fast.

170

Ahmed ran away from Jones. Penders began shooting in the direction of the mysterious sniper. Jones took her gun and decided to aim at Adam Aarons! Bret Stevens then jumped in front of the boy and took the bullet on the right side of the chest. I ran in a circular flank of Mr. Penders, who was still shooting at Noto. I then tacked him from the side and knocked the gun from his hands. I turned around to protect everyone from Ms. Jones but she was gone!

"Mark, Mark!" yelled Noto as she jumped down from the tree and ran in my direction. I cuffed Penders as the rest of the FBI and state police finally arrived at our location. We tended to Stevens who had a hole in the side of his chest and was breathing heavily.

"I feel so badly at what a mess I've made of my life!" he rasped.

"Hang in there," I said. "Paramedics are on their way. They're being flown in." However, I knew deep down the odds of him surviving were very slim. So, I whispered to him "I will tell everyone about how you saved Adam's life. I believe God will forgive you for your sins."

Steven's eyes penetrated mine and I felt a certain level of peace in them. He had had a very difficult several years and I'm sure in some ways, it was a blessing to be leaving this life.

"Please just tell me where the flash drive is of the evidence you have against the Gochies and Principal Lodewyk. Tell me what you can and I will do what I can to clear your name."

Chapter 20

The forest outside the small town of Cedarville, Maine, was a true circus. Medical choppers flew in the E.M.S., more law enforcement, social services agencies and even the media all came pouring into get the initial scoop on the breaking news about the boys being found. The families of Adam Aaron, Kenny VanderPlaats, and Ronald Meacham were notified and were being flown in by the FBI. Even the families of the local teenagers, Ahmed Mehta and Tim O'Malley, were notified. Most of the personnel had to fly in by helicopter because of the complexity of navigating through this forest amidst the labyrinth of paths. The rescued boys were being given morphine to keep them calm after their traumatic experience. We gave the medics their medications that we had confiscated from the boys' captivity. It was a relief that Bret Stevens and the kidnappers had accessed information about their medications so they could properly take care of the boys. The boys were being air lifted to the hospital to be checked for injuries and to undergo tests. Ronald Meacham had had a seizure after Betty Jones had kicked him full force in the stomach. Medical attention was a necessity for him since he was ill equipped to deal with such violence. The social worker who had arrived at the scene had demanded that we not ask any questions of the boys at this time, but to first re-unite them with their families. Tim O'Malley had already told me about how he and his buddy Ahmed had stumbled upon the boys being chased and all they had been through. Although he claimed that he had no injuries, he agreed to be flown to the hospital to be checked out. If nothing else, he could assist in helping the three boys and with the recovery of Ahmed, who had suffered a broken nose because of Betty Jones.

As for the criminals, Bret Stevens took his last breath shortly after divulging the information about the info about the Gochies. He was pronounced dead at the scene and airlifted to the hospital to be placed in the morgue. Rick Penders was cuffed and was so far, not talking but demanding to speak to a lawyer. It was likely that since he was former military, the army would confiscate him and probably lock him up in a military stockade. The problem was we still had to interview him. There was so much we had to know such as how he had hacked into the schools' firewalls and gained access to the boys' confidential information. We also wanted to know how they had gotten supplies and food to this hidden building, the flash grenades, tasers, etc. Also, since he had been a former CIA employee; that too would complicate things. Inter-agency cooperation did not always exist in this country as it probably should.

As for Betty Jones, she had escaped and was at-large. How she had navigated her way out of the forest and past the stonewall of FBI and other law enforcement that had converged upon this forest was anybody's guess. There was a BOLO out on her and there would certainly be a national if not international manhunt for this woman. Not only was she a mercenary and serial killer, but also the one who had kidnapped and nearly murdered three boys with special needs. Public outrage would be high and many would probably not rest until she was caught and brought to justice. I knew I wouldn't!

After the boys had been airlifted, I grabbed a Pepsi from the FBI cooler and sought out my friend, Jen Noto.

"Man, the fatigue and stress of the last few days in definitely catching up to me. I need a three-day nap!"

"Yeah, I could probably use one too," said Noto. "Well, now I have the time now that I lost my job as a reporter."

"Are you regretting your decision?" I asked her.

"No, not a chance," she said. "I really enjoyed being able to help with this search and do some real good."

"Even though it put your life in danger?"

"Yeah, I amazingly am not overly stressed about that danger. I had to be thick skinned and brave since I was a reporter..."

"Yeah, especially since you pissed a lot of people off, including me," I added now in a humorous way. I was finding it now a lot easier to forgive this woman.

"You're right," said Noto. "I certainly feel a great deal of shame with my past mistakes and ethical corners cut. Hopefully this case was somewhat of a penance."

"I think it was," I said since she had saved my life today and had saved me from getting a severe beating just days earlier.

"Well, like I said, I think I need a few days to relax, and then I will continue making difficult life decisions."

***

Andrew Aaron's heart pounded as he anticipated this reunion with his twin brother. Right now, this was turning into the best day of his life. The fear he had felt the last few days thinking he might never see his brother again was indescribable. In addition to knowing he would soon see his brother again, he was getting to ride in an FBI jet! Cool! As the family was escorted into the hospital, Andrew braced himself for seeing Adam again.

"He's been sleeping for a while," said the nurse. "I'll let you decide if you want to wake him."

As they entered the room, Andrew broke down crying. He had cried more the past few days than he had in probably two years. However, most of his tears the past few days had been out of fear.

"Andrew!" said Adam.

"Adam!" all three of them said as Adam jumped out of the bed in his green hospital robe and ran to his family.

Andrew clung hard to his brother wanting to never let go again. Andrew did another thing he had not done in a couple of years: he kissed his brother on the cheek.

"PlayStation?" asked Adam.

Andrew beamed and answered, "Anything you want buddy!" Andrew marveled at how the first thing his brother thought about was the PlayStation in Andrew's room. Adam always wanted to play it and his parents had always forced Andrew to let him allow his brother to play. Sometimes, Adam was only allowed to play the system for good behavior. Andrew looked forward to not only playing PlayStation with his brother, but spending much more quality time with him for now on!

***

In the rooms of the other boys, similar reunions were taking place. Andrea, Tyler and Brittney Meacham entered the room down the hall where Ronald was resting. Despite his low cognitive ability, Ronald was no dummy. He would never forget his family and was relieved to see them. He too began crying, which he did not do very often, and hugged his parents and sister. Ronald still felt pain from where the woman had kicked him in the stomach with super speed. However, he did not think about the pain as he was so happy to see his family!

Brittney embraced Ronald in a full bear hug and the two hugged while tears ran down their faces. The siblings stood there not wanting to let go of each other. Brittney said through her sobbing voice "Ron, I will never be embarrassed to have you as a brother again! I also promise to protect you and take care of you for the rest of our lives!"

In the next room, The VanderPlaats were overwhelmed with joy in seeing their son again.

"Oh my gosh, I think you've grown!" said Mr. VanderPlaats to Kenny as the boy hugged them fiercely.

"No, you've gotten smaller," said Kenny.

They all laughed as they could tell Kenny had not lost his sense of humor.

***

Seeing the reunions thoroughly warmed my heart. The parents of all three boys thanked me thoroughly. Even Tyler Meacham, whom I had investigated a year earlier for his gambling and money laundering scandal, was very thankful. Sometimes it took a tragedy of this magnitude of having a son kidnapped to make one change their ways and have a healthier outlook. We truly don't know what we have until we've lost it. Unfortunately, my experience with my wife and daughter had not had a happy ending.

***

Tim O'Malley sat by the bed of his best friend, Ahmed Mehta. Ahmed was very tired from the painkillers the hospital had given him and was currently sleeping. His friend had shown a lot of courage and growth during the past several hours. He had always teased his friend for not taking charge enough, but he would not do that anymore. Tim and Ahmed's parents were sitting outside. Tim's mom could not believe what he had been through and had hugged him fiercely.

"Mom, I'm fine!" he had said.

"Yeah, but learning that my baby almost died earlier today has me a little shaken!"

Tim had rolled his eyes like he often did with his parents, but he certainly understood where she was coming from.

"You'll understand when you have kids someday," his mom said. "Anyway, I am so proud of you for what you did today by protecting your friend and the three missing boys! Who would have thought they were in our community!"

Once Adam got over his teenage ego, he decided it was time to give his mom a compliment.

"Mom, it was your talent that got me through today," Tim said. "Everything you taught me about what you do as a special needs teacher helped me. I have a new level of respect for what you do."

Mrs. O'Malley hugged him and again informed him of how much she loved him and was proud of him.

After she left him to remain with his best friend, he actually began crying. He reflected on how he had at times bullied kids with special needs when he was in middle school. He had not understood them and thought they seemed weird. Other than that, he wasn't really sure why he had occasionally picked on them. It just kind of seemed like his right as an athletic kid to keep those "weird" kids in their place. How stupid he had been! In a way, he guessed it was partially because he had wanted to rebel against his mom, the special ed teacher. He had been raised as a Christian and now realized that it was his sinful nature that had caused him to rebel and reject his parents' teaching. As he sat there in the hospital room, he looked up to the ceiling and silently prayed to God. Even though he had accepted Jesus a few years earlier, he re-asked Jesus into his heart and to forgive him for his sins, especially for the bullying from a younger age. He even felt guilty for how he sometimes teased Ahmed and some of his other friends. He had meant it in a good-natured way, but sometimes his teasing was mean spirited and inappropriate. He would work on that area also. Tim also realized that it surely had been divine intervention that had caused him and Ahmed to build the fort in the woods that had enabled them to hide and protect Ronald, Adam and Kenny. He then vowed to dedicate his life to being a positive influence for kids with special needs. In fact, now he was quite certain he would do what a couple of years earlier he had vowed he would not do: follow in his mom's footsteps and become a special education teacher.

He then walked over to where Ahmed lie and gripped the hand of his sleeping friend. "You're going to be ok buddy!"

Soon after that, the parents of the three rescued boys wanted to personally thank him for protecting their kids. Then FBI Agent Mark Graham sat down with him and asked him a few final questions to wrap up the case.

Chapter 21

The next few weeks, things settled into a more normal routine for me. There was a lot of paperwork and other things to do to close the case. The FBI techs stayed in the abandoned warehouse for several days and continued to analyze evidence and research the "how-they-dunnit" as kidnappers. The search continued to go on for Betty Jones but she had indeed escaped. Chances were she was out of the country by now.

"Well, at least we found the kids. That's the important thing," Jen Noto reminded
me.

"You're right," I said. "I just wish we could have gotten her also. The fact that she apparently had no problem with killing the three boys with special needs just pisses me off. I don't like the idea of her being out there with an opportunity to hurt more kids!"

Rumor had it that the homecomings of the three boys were awesome. Each classroom had parties for them. Apparently a few Hollywood producers had approached the families about movie deals for their kids' stories, but thank goodness the families had declined. Even I had told the producers to take a hike when they had asked me the same thing. It sure didn't seem right to benefit financially from this scary time when the only payment we really wanted and needed was the satisfaction of the kids being returned safely.

Penders had indeed been taken to a maximum security military prison. So far, I had interviewed him a couple of times and gained insight into his hacking abilities. Unfortunately, much of the technical jargon was over my head. He still could not believe that Adam Aaron had gotten past his block in order to send an email to his school.

After work one of the evenings, I had made arrangements to have Jen Noto and my daughter, Michelle, at my house for dinner. Michelle agreed to bring lasagna since my culinary talents were fairly limited to spaghetti, frozen dinners and other bachelor meals. Jen agreed to bring a salad and some cooled white Chardonnay.

"Wow, your townhouse is quite attractive," said Noto. "You are quite a guy
working full-time and maintaining such a beautiful interior design."

"Well, thank you for giving me a reason to clean and straighten up the place!"

"Hey, don't be fooled," said Michelle to Jen. "This place still needs a woman's touch."

Leave it to my daughter to subtly and yet, not so subtly, communicate her wishes!

I laughed uneasily, but Jen did not seem shy about my daughter's suggestion.

Well, I'd be happy to spend more time with your dad and enhance his décor," Noto said while winking to me.

I blushed and almost felt like a 14-year old again.

The two women hit it off very well. We talked little about the case but more about politics, sports and other goings-on in the news. I definitely enjoyed spending time with Jen Noto and needed to decide how to proceed with her. In truth, I still was not completely over Sharon. Perhaps, I never would be completely. However, it was important that I at some point move on and let some other woman into my heart. Hopefully, that day would come soon.

After the night concluded and we said our goodbyes, I made final arrangements to travel with Agent Jonathon Sparks back to Illinois to retrieve the flash drive that the dying Stevens had informed us of. This piece of hardware was the reason everything had happened. It contained whatever evidence Stevens had of the Gochies and Principal Lodewyk. Our hunch after Sparks had spoken to Steven's mom, was that Stevens had wanted to use this evidence to ruin Suzie Gochie. Mr. Gochie obviously was doing whatever he

180

could to hush Stevens, who had this flash drive. After clearing bureaucratic hurdles, we finally had the green light to go ahead and search the residence where Stevens had whispered to me about where he had hidden the flash drive. Hopefully, this would provide the evidence we needed to go after Mr. Gochie's daughter, Dr. Lodewyk and hopefully, Mr. Gochie himself.

***

The next day, we were in Grover Ups, Illinois, and Sparks and I approached the house that used to belong to Bret Stevens and his mom. The current owners were not overly happy about having their house being searched by the FBI, but they had little choice. We entered and began searching in a room that looked like was currently a study or computer room for the current residents. Stevens had said in his dying breath that he had hidden the flash drive under the laminate wooden floor in a bedroom right next to the downstairs bathroom. We searched and searched but all the floorboards seemed fairly sturdy. Was it possible that Stevens had been wrong? Had he lied to us to throw us off? After all, he had been evil enough to orchestrate the kidnapping plan. Maybe to some extent he had faked his remorse in order to get a lighter punishment. Well, I didn't really think so. My B.S. meter was pretty high and I got no negative signals when Stevens finally broke down. However, I was pretty stressed in that situation considering the man was holding Adam Aaron hostage. Nonetheless, Sparks and I continued our search and were about to give up when I noticed a squeaking sound below my feet. The two of us reached down and began pushing on the loose board. It finally loosened and we were able to pull it out of the floor! Finally, I reached inside and pulled out a light-colored flash drive being contained inside a dusty plastic bag. So this was it! This was the hardware that apparently had incriminating evidence against the billionaire Mr. Gochie's daughter and perhaps him as well. This was why Mr. Gochie had paid mega millions of dollars to Bret Stevens. Stevens had threatened to expose the daughter, who had gotten him fired as a special education teacher. Stevens had used that hush money to fund his crazy and delusional plan to make himself a teacher again. Sometimes humanity clearly scared me!

As I lifted the bag out of the opening, I raised my head and noticed Sparks pointing a gun at me! There was just something about having a gun pointed at my head that always gets my heartbeat pounding a million beats a minute despite my training. Forcing myself to remain calm, I said "Ok, am I under arrest or something?"

"Hand over the flash drive!" said Sparks.

Chapter 22

"Yeah sure," I said. "If you wanted to have it to get the credit for finding it, all you had to do was ask."

Sparks gave a weak smile. "Hey, money truly talks man. Ten million dollars from Mr. Gochie!"

I nodded as it all fell into place. "So, you've been bought. After 40 years as an agent, you've been bought. Good job man!"

"Hey, don't try to put a guilt trip on me!" said Sparks as he glared at me. "I've put in 40 years and have not been appreciated. I've been passed over for promotion so many times! Despite all I've done, what really changes man!?"

"So why not just take the money, right?" I asked sarcastically.

"Don't act so innocent Graham!" he said, as he tightened his grip, shoved the gun inches from my head and seemed as if he were on the verge of pulling the trigger. "You would not have turned down that kind of money if Mr. Gochie had offered it to you?"

"I guess I measure success and fulfilment differently than you do," I said.

"Don't lecture me or try to reason with me," said Sparks. "I've done my job well and Mr. Gochie offered me a better payday than what Uncle Sam ever offered. Now it is time for me to kill you."

"How are you going to get away with this?" I asked in a slightly trembling voice wanting to keep him talking.

He laughed. "Hey, I've got one of the richest men in the world backing me in this little endeavor."

I shuttered knowing that having a billionaire like Gochie in your corner was a very strong card to play.

"He has so many cops in his payroll that we can easily make your body disappear. After you die, he has arranged to have several cops come over to 'assist us' in our search and will quietly escort your body out of here. The owners already have been taken away from the house so they won't see that I am leaving without the agent I entered with. I am then going to make the statement to the press and the FBI that you had a breakdown."

"A breakdown?" I asked confused.

Sparks then chuckled a bit.

"Yes, you are the grieving man who lost his wife and daughter."

I felt a rush of rage surge through me since Sparks had the nerve to bring my deceased wife and daughter into this! I wanted to lunge at him, but he still had a gun fixated on me. My opportunity to take him down was not here yet.

"I haven't decided if I am going to say you committed suicide or just left. Probably that you just left and disappeared forever. Your family and other agents would get suspicious if we claimed you had died but we didn't have a body. They will have less trouble accepting that your guilt and misery over not being able to protect them that fateful night led you to disappear and start over."

"My son and daughter will never believe that!"

Sparks shrugged indifferently. "Still, there will be no evidence that we are lying. They will eventually just have to accept what we are saying."

He smirked. "Have I left anything out?"

I shrugged. "Yeah, just one thing."

"What's that?" asked a now impatient and irritated Sparks.

"We were right about our hunch about you."

"What!?"

Since I now had him by the window, I said "Fire!"

A shocked Sparks' eyes widened, as he pulled the trigger just as a sniper round nailed him in his stomach, and I dove out of the way. Sparks dropped the gun, I grabbed it, kicked Spark's feet out from under him and soon the house was invaded by cops and FBI agents.

184

As we handcuffed a wounded and bleeding Agent Sparks, I shrugged and said to him the old cliché, "Keep your friends close, and your enemies closer."

***

Agent Jonathon Sparks had been under suspicion for a long time by the FBI. We knew he had been bitter about being passed over for promotion and seemed to have mentally, checked out. Even though he still was a good agent and did his job fairly well, we just figured something was off. He had been under investigation and other agents had been following him but were never able to find anything incriminating against him. We had suspected that he had taken bribes in other cases, but had no proof. Who knows, maybe Sparks had been truthful about turning down the initial bribe from Gochie, but the old man had finally gotten to this morally loose and frustrated agent. My supervisor and I figured that Sparks may have been vulnerable to being bought since Gochie was who he was and certainly had the motive and desire to use his money to protect his daughter using whatever means necessary. So, with the backing of FBI Director Scheelhaase, we had agreed to let Sparks go with me to retrieve this flash drive figuring if he had indeed been bought, our time alone in the house would have been the best opportunity for him to reveal his true colors and make his move. That's why I was wired and we had numerous agents surrounding the house, just in case.

So, things moved quickly after this incident. Fortunately, Gochie was not able to penetrate our agency as well as he thought he had, and the flash drive was an absolute game changer for the entire investigation. This small piece of hardware began with a video of Stevens himself explaining his situation. Suzanne had apparently bragged about how she and her father owned half the town and could get anyone hired or fired. She also joked about how they were above the law. Even though Stevens, an idealistic special education teacher, had initially been thrilled to date the daughter of one of the wealthiest men in America, this reveal on her part had obviously pissed off his conscious. She had been cocky and showed him this flash drive that apparently had pictures and even all the bookkeeping, accounting of Mr. Gochie's underworld empire. Even though we were close in our hunches, there apparently was not evidence of an affair between Principal Lodewyk and Ms. Gochie. Stevens had simply wanted to break up with her because of her low morals. Suzanne Gochie, the spurned lover, had then apparently bribed Lodewyk to fire Stevens. Since Stevens was obsessed with teaching, he had broken into Ms. Gochie's car and taken the flash drive out of her glove compartment, which she had apparently previously bragged to him about how she kept their bookkeeping records and other financial deals. He had taken the flash drive, disappeared and extorted numerous millions if they did not pay him. We knew that there had to have been some VERY incriminating evidence if Gochie would have paid Stevens that much money. As the FBI continued to dig through the files of the flash drive, there were documents of him doing business with Tony Connelli! Tony was the brother of Louie Connelli. While Louie ran the family business in Augusta, Maine, Tony was in charge of the business operations in Chicago. This was a humorous coincidence since I had interviewed Louie Connelli for being involved in the kidnapping initially of Ronald Meacham. Even though Connelli had no real connection with this caper, he was loosely connected in a roundabout way. Hah, this partially explained why Gochie was afraid of the flash drive info getting exposed to the public. If the flash drive got to the right authorities or the media, it would not only ruin Gochie's underground corporate empire and other powerful people, it would also get him in trouble with the mob. Even billionaire Thomas Gochie was afraid of mob bosses Louie and Tony Connelli. Further documents showed business dealings and

186

other major bribery deals with politicians from Washington. The scandal was going to lead to numerous hearings and other legal proceedings involving members of the highest levels of government. It turned out the millions of dollars of extortion money paid to Stevens would have been less than the millions of dollars paid in legal fees to Gochie's and the major politicians' legal fees and high priced lawyers.

The evidence was showcased on all the major news outlets, and Mr. Gochie and his corporation were ruined. Plus, we were able to arrest him since he had clearly bribed Sparks as made evident in Spark's confession to me. Sparks even ratted out the corrupt cops and FBI agents that he knew of.

Yes, it was scary that Mr. Gochie quite possibly had numerous local cops and clearly had a few feds in his pocket. Plus, the trial was going to be a long and drawn out process. Mr. Gochie clearly had the best lawyers that money could buy. However, this case hopefully truly showed that most of us in law enforcement and other positions within the government are basically good people. Thankfully the age-old cliché that good overcomes evil is this time, true.

***

Noto and I sat at an IHOP eating scrambled eggs, bacon and hash browns as she and I reminisced about the case.
"How does it feel knowing that you helped return the boys to their families?" asked Noto as she sprinkled salt on her food.

"It feels great," I said with a dismissive shrug.

Noto raised her eyebrows and shot him a double take look. "You don't seem all that sincere," she responded.

"Dang woman, I'm supposed to be the expert at reading people."

"Hey, I used to be a reporter, don't forget. Part of my job was reading people and uncovering the truth based on what they said. Plus, there is a little thing called a woman's intuition that I have going for me."

"Touché," I exclaimed. "Oh, all right Ms. Freud, here it is: I cannot get my wife and daughter out of my head!"

Noto gently reached across the table and gently held my hand. "I don't blame you Mark; that is a tragedy nobody could easily get over."

"Well, it's not so much that I can't get over them anymore, it also has to do with the fact that their killer is still out there and quite possibly being cared for in a hospital. If Armon Luck really is their killer, I want him in a real prison, not a hospital! Plus, there are too many other loose ends in this case. I really feel that I need to know why Sharon agreed to meet Armon Luck in private. There have to be text messages or some electronic trail we can follow up on!"

"I hear you, my friend! I just don't see how we can re-open the case when the new evidence about the hidden passageway was discovered by illegal means."

"Maybe it's time we do a little more sleuthing around the institution," I said.

Noto then placed her fork down after swallowing and rested her chin on top of both of her raised hands. "Wow, it seems as if I am really corrupting you rather than you making an honest person out of me. Sneaking around and using questionable ethics is usually my game!"

"I'm serious! I know nothing we find will probably hold up in court, but I have to know just for my own peace of mind!"

"Ok, but what exactly do you have in mind?" asked Noto. "I don't think I can re- enter the hospital with my ruse of being Armon Luck's sister again. Plus, if you are caught going to the hospital, won't they recognize you?"

"I'm not planning on us going into the hospital," I said.

Noto eyed me with an expression that begged me to continue.

"No, I think we need to talk to the nurse, Anne Potocki," I said.

"Seriously? How can we approach her without being on official duty?" asked Noto.

"We do it unofficially and we follow her home," I said.

"Mark, I'm not liking this one bit. Your grief is more than most people have to cope with, so I'm not going to say I know what you are going through. But if you following this woman, who may have played a role in your family's murder, home, you may do something you seriously regret. You are going off the deep end. I feel that I have to report this to Mr. Bingham. You are jeopardizing not only your career, but also your freedom by going rogue like this!"

I pursed my lips. A part of me wanted to play hardball with this woman right now; this same woman whom I had hated for years and had considered an evil sleaze. Yet here she was now being the voice of reason. I was thinking irrationally since there seemed to be nothing in the realm of the law that I could do to bring justice to Sharon and Angela. I could probably threaten her right now or tell her to mind her own business. However, that would not be right. She truly cared for me now and was looking out for me more than I was.

"You are right, Jen. I have to accept things as they are and move on with my life. Nothing good can come from following Anne Potocki. Thank you for threatening to report me."

"Hey, what are friends for?" asked Noto.

Epilogue

Three months later, I was invited to dinner at the Aarons' house. As I drove to their home, I reflected on the events of the last few months. Mr. Gochie had been indicted on a charge of federal corruption and bribery charges. He was currently on bail and his lawyers were working hard to arrange a settlement with the state and U.S. Department of Justice. There was a huge chance that he would avoid any hard time because of his vast resources and wealth. Well, at least the stock in his corporation had plummeted and his public image was at an all-time low. His daughter had been extradited back to the United States for her role in the bribery scandal and too was on trial. It turned out she had simply been a spurned lover and had been dumped by Stevens. That was why she had asked Principal Lodewyk to fire him. Stevens had then stolen the flash drive with the vast incriminating information that would ruin Gochie, his corporate empire and burn other high level politicians. Ms. Gochie explained that her father wanted to have Stevens eliminated or at least intimidated by the mafia so he could stop paying the extortion money. She explained that she felt somewhat guilty for ruining Steven's career so that was why she begged her father not to hurt him.

"I never really stopped loving him!" said a tearful Gochie.

As for my life, things had gotten back to fairly normal; back to my semi-mundane existence. There was truly no way I could ever get over my wife and daughter, at least I didn't think so. When the time is right, I will somehow find a way to find out what happened to my wife and daughter. For now, Jen Noto and I had talked about dating. There was clearly a strong connection there, but I just wasn't quite ready to date or love again. She said she understood and would wait until I was ready.

I pulled into the Aarons' driveway and was greeted with open arms by Alice and Ben Aaron.

"Mark, it is so good to have you over," said the cheerful and warm Alice Aaron. "Thank you again for returning our boy to us!"

"It was my pleasure ma'am! I was simply doing my job."

After a few more minutes of pleasantries, she called to her twin boys who were supposedly engaged in an intense game of Call of Duty.

Adam ran into the living room and seemed to be in a good mood. Alice Aaron said to him "Adam, do you know who this is?"

Adam paused and then began scripting some movie.

"Adam, this is Mr. Graham. Say 'Hi Mr. Graham.'"

"Hi Mr. Graham," said Adam.

Even Andrew seemed a little shy at first, but then he began talking about how relieved he was to have his brother back safe again.

"It was hard for a while, man. I did not want to let Adam be in his classroom by himself for the first several days."

The Aarons shared about how overall Adam was adjusting quite well despite the post-traumatic stress. However, he would sometimes wake up in the middle of the night screaming thinking he was back at that other school. He was seeing a social worker, but since Adam had such a high level of autism, he was not able to articulate his feelings as clearly as someone else would. They had him draw pictures on the computer to express his feelings about his experience.

Throughout the dinner, Adam went about his echolalia, which is when kids with autism script speech that is not relevant to the current situation. Twice at dinner, Adam said something that triggered something in the depths of my mind. Then he said it again, "Send the deposit to the Raiffeisen in Switzerland account number 3333-4555." What was it he was saying? Switzerland, the Raiffeisen, account number 3333-4555? I spaced out as I reflected on what he might be saying. Suddenly it hit me like a nuclear explosion and I almost spit my wine out!

"That's it!" I exclaimed.

"What's it?" asked a confused and perplexed Andrew Aaron while both the parents, Ben and Alice, also looked at him expectantly. "I think what he just said was a vital clue!" I exclaimed excitedly. Andrew and his father looked at each other puzzled and then directed their gazes back to me.

"He's actually been saying that on and off since he's been home," said Alice. "We figured it was just a quote from a movie or something he heard in a conversation. He often remembers random quotes and sayings from his life and recites them whenever and out of context."

To be polite, I finished dinner. However, then I immediately called for Travis Bingham.

***

Betty Jones sipped her strawberry margarita, as she enjoyed another day on the beach in Turks and Caicos. The payout she had received from Bret Stevens had worked out and this would be a nice way to spend her retirement. Even though she was still fairly young and missed the thrill of battle and various other mercenary missions, this was a pretty awesome existence. She still felt bitter at that FBI agent and those two teenagers for robbing her of the opportunity to complete the mission with the three boys. She did not like leaving any loose ends. Maybe someday life would give her a chance to get even with them, but for now, this *was* the life.

After soaking up the sun, she decided she would head back to her house and order some food. Then she would take a nap and perhaps go snorkeling later in the day.

192

She ordered her room service, turned on a showing of "Pirates of the Caribbean, "and waited for her food. She heard a knock on the door and went to answer it. She was starving! The food service worker had a cart with her food on it. However, there was something different about this food service worker. Sure, he did not have dark skin like most of the residents and workers down here. yet he still seemed eerily familiar to her. Since she was not one for small talk, she began to pay the man the tip.

"You owe me a lot more than that," the man said.

"What are you talking about?" said an impatient Betty Jones.

"You owe me some time in prison."

Betty's eyes widened as she realized what was going on. She tried to run away but FBI agent Mark Graham pulled his gun on her. Just then, Agent Ken Thompson and two other agents converged upon her and began cuffing her.

***

"**M**s. Jones," I said. "You have the right to remain silent! Anything you say can and will be used against you in a court of law. We are arresting you on the charges of being involved in the kidnapping of Ronald Meacham, Adam Aaron and Kenny VanderPlaats. You are also being charged in the murder of Bret Stevens and assault towards Ahmed Mehta and Ronald Meacham. We've also got you for attempting to murder the three kidnapped victims and Tim O'Malley. You are returning to the States with us where you will answer for all of these charges."

"How the heck did you find me!!???" asked an understandably shocked Betty Jones.

"Well, here is the deal," I said while pushing the food cart out of the way and standing directly in front of her. "You really had underestimated the kids that you kidnapped, especially the boy with autism. You just have to be extremely careful what you say around them. Kids with autism tend to remember and file almost everything they hear and often repeat it during random moments."

"What are you talking about?" snarled Jones.

"Does the Raiffeisen in Switzerland mean anything to you? I asked. "Account number 3333-4555?"

Ms. Jones' face turned from anger to one of complete shock.

"Yes, you apparently mentioned your off-shore account where you send your money when Adam Aaron was present. I'm guessing you were on your phone authorizing the transferring of the money."

Betty Jones then remembered making that call while she was watching Adam Aaron on the computer.

"You see, I remembered Bret Stevens mentioning sending money to Swiss bank accounts shortly before he died. After Adam revealed the account number and the Raiffeisen bank in Switzerland, we were able to track your account down to Zurich, Switzerland. Well, then it was just a matter of doing detective work. With the bank's cooperation, we discovered where all you withdrew money. We tracked your steps down here and customs was very helpful in helping us locate you at this condo. I have to hand it to you, you are very good at what you do. The way you eluded all of us in Maine was quite impressive. However, what comes around goes around."

***

After we hauled Betty Jones away as she cussed and threatened us, I felt that the case was truly over. I was slightly disappointed that I could not spend more time in Turks and Caicos for the weather was now pretty lousy on the East Coast. Turks and Caicos would be a nice place to have a family reunion. Once Michelle and Aiden had their own kids, maybe I would bring all of them down here for a family reunion at one of the all-inclusive resorts. From what I've heard, they have extensive activities and programs for kids. However, it would be painful not having Sharon down there with me to be part of it. Should I include Jen Noto in such a family function? Speaking of her, I had not spoken with her in several days. Just then, I felt an overwhelming need to talk to her. So I picked up my Samsung Galaxy S-5 phone and gave her a call.

The End